W9-BEX-165

WAR BROTHERS

WAR BROTHERS

THE NOVEL

SHARON E. McKAY

Cover art by Daniel Lafrance
Designed by Monica Charny

First edition published in 2008 by Puffin Canada

Annick Press Ltd.

We acknowledge the support of the Canada Council for the Arts, the Ontario Arts Council, and the Government of Canada through the Canada Book Fund (CBF) for our publishing activities.

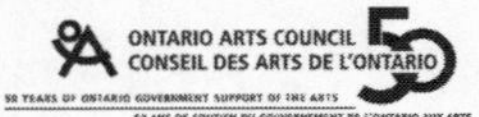

Cataloging in Publication

McKay, Sharon E., author
War brothers : the novel / Sharon E. McKay.
Originally published: Toronto : Puffin, 2008.
ISBN 978-1-55451-648-3 (bound).--ISBN 978-1-55451-647-6 (pbk.)
I. Title.
PS8575.K2898W37 2014 jC813'.6 C2013-906981-X

Published in the U.S.A. by
Annick Press (U.S.) Ltd.

Distributed in the U.S.A. by
Firefly Books (U.S.) Inc.
P.O. Box 1338
Ellicott Station
Buffalo, NY 14205

Printed in Canada

Visit us at: www.annickpress.com
Visit Sharon E. McKay at: www.sharonmckay.com

Also available in e-book format. Please visit www.annickpress.com/ebooks.html for more details. Or scan

Barbara Berson, friends walking forward

This is a work of fiction based on accurate events that continue today

"Poyo too pe rweny."
"Death is a scar that never heals."
—ACHOLI SAYING

"In each of us there is the possibility to be a beast, but also the possibility to reach the stars."
—ELEANOR ROOSEVELT

CONTENTS

	Dear Reader	xiii
1	Jacob	1
2	The Night Commuters	12
3	Oteka	19
4	Medicine Man	29
5	School Days	34
6	America and Bull's Blood	39
7	Abduction	50
8	Punishment by Death	56
9	Tony	61
10	God	70
11	*Nyuma Geuka*	74
12	Two Weeks Later	81
13	ATTACK!	89
14	*Cen*—Evil Spirits	97
15	Hannah	103

CONTENTS

16 Little Girls 108
17 Kony 115
18 Norman Will Die 122
19 The Lion's Claw 134
20 Lizard 144
21 One Shot 149
22 The Crocodile and the Scorpion 155
23 Returnees 159
24 A Lie for the Truth 165
25 The Nature of the Beast 170
Dear Reader 179
Afterword by Adrian Bradbury, founder of GuluWalk 185
Glossary 187
Acknowledgments 191

AFRICA
SUDAN
UGANDA
Gulu
Kampala
DEMOCRATIC
REPUBLIC
OF THE
CONGO
KENYA

GULU, UGANDA, 2009

Dear Reader,

My name is Kitino Jacob. I was born in Gulu, a city of 110,000 people in the north of Uganda. I am from the Acholi tribe.

Where I live, far from the capital city of Kampala, Kony Joseph leads the Lord's Resistance Army (or the LRA). My country knows this man simply as Kony, the leader of an army of abducted children. He and his LRA gang of rebels steal boys and girls from rural farms, villages, schools, and buses. They say that only they know the true Christian way, that their army of Christian soldiers will fight the government of Uganda and create a country of Christians called "Acholiland." But Kony and his Lord's Resistance Army are cruel beyond measure. They are not Christians. They do not care for or protect children. I know this to be true because I was one of those abducted children. I became a child soldier in Kony's army.

My story is not an easy one to tell, and it is not an easy one to read. The life of a child soldier is full of unthinkable violence and brutal death. But this is also a story of hope, courage, friendship, and family. We Ugandans believe that family is most important.

I thought you should be prepared for both the bad and the good. There is no shame in closing this book now.

Jacob

1
JACOB

Gulu, 2002

Jacob dodged; he weaved, he pulled back a bare foot and followed through. The football bounced off the side wall of his house. He leapt up to the applause of thousands while catching the ball on the rebound. With the skill of a top player from Manchester United—the roughest, the toughest, the best team in the world—he tossed the ball behind him, then chased it. Arms tucked close and legs spinning as fast as a sewing machine, he was Cristiano Ronaldo coming up the middle. *Flying*. SCORE! *Yes, yes*. He waved to the cheering crowd.

"Jacob!" A voice yelled from the drive. Jacob spun around and waved to Lakony Tony.

A sleepy guard, propping himself up with his toy-like gun, staggered out of the little hut that stood at the entrance to the family compound as the boy approached. He looked Tony up and down, shrugged, and waved him inside.

"Jacob, over here!"

Tony dropped his homemade rag ball and ran full tilt toward Jacob's leather football. Jacob kicked the ball toward Tony. With one, two moves, Tony booted it toward the wall of the house again, knocking off bits of stucco. SCORE! *The crowd goes mad!* If Jacob was Cristiano Ronaldo, then Tony was Thierry Henry.

Head bent, focused, Jacob charged the ball. "Go! Go!" yelled the guard.

Jacob faked a kick, then ducked behind Tony and came up the inside. Pull back, SCORE! The guard cheered and Tony moaned.

"Jacob," Ethel called from the doorway. Two green glass bottles of Krest clinked in her hands.

Ethel was father's third cousin and the housekeeper, but sometimes she behaved as though she owned the house. She had long legs and wore a *busutis*, a traditional wrap-around dress that fell to her ankles. Her head was shaved. "Long hair is a nuisance," she had said many, many times.

Jacob gave the ball a last kick. A bounce off the wall upset a lizard perched on the windowsill. It flashed a forked tongue, then raced up the wall toward the roof.

Ethel popped off the caps with a bottle opener, then passed the bottles out with a stern look. "Your father is expecting guests. Please, no more noise."

Both boys slumped down, backs against the wall of the house, knees up, and drank their sodas. Tony sipped his slowly. A soda drink was common enough in Jacob's house, but not where Tony came from. The slums of Gulu, where Tony lived, were only blocks from Jacob's big house, but really, it might as well have been a different world.

Jacob's house was part of a large compound, surrounded by a two-metre high wall. Inside the wall were many buildings: one for storage, one for servants, and a guest house too. The main house was painted lemon yellow and trimmed in light blue, the color of a clear sky at midday. The roof was made of iron but it was badly rusted and now dripped a gritty red when the rains came.

"Father must take the car to Kampala. I will go to school by bus tomorrow," announced Jacob. "So we will go together."

Jacob did not mind taking the bus, but driving in the car was really much more fun. He liked the cold air that poured out of the automobile's vents. Tony had said that the cold air was for whites, because, just as they needed to drink water from bottles and smear cream on their skin to prevent it from turning black, they needed cool air to breathe properly.

"Who are they?" Tony pointed to five—no, six—distinguished men walking past the guard's hut toward the front door. Ethel greeted each one on the steps of the house.

"I do not know them all, but that one is Okumu Adam, and the man behind him is Musa Henry Torac, father's oldest friend." Jacob took another big swig of soda and watched Musa Henry Torac shuffle along the path. Everyone knew that he had lost two sons to *twoo jonyo* AIDS, and his daughters-in-law and four grandchildren, too. Jacob had overheard Ethel and old Bella, the cook, whispering about it. No one spoke of it, not out loud. To die of *twoo jonyo* AIDS was to die in shame.

Musa Henry Torac stopped and gazed toward the boys.

"*Woda*, my boys, come." He lifted a heavy hand and waved.

Both boys leapt up and ran, stopping just short of crashing into the old man.

"I see how you have grown, Jacob. How old are you now?" Musa Henry Torac looked at the boy with affection. His face was worn with deep lines like a river gone dry, but his eyes were as bright as a child's.

"I am fourteen," Jacob said proudly.

"Well then, you will be thinking of your future, of university, perhaps. What subjects do you like?"

"He likes mathematics," Tony piped up, then stopped. It was very rude to interrupt. "I mean, Jacob is the best at multiplying in our whole school. He can multiply anything." Tony looked at Jacob with pride.

"Mathematics, is it?" Musa Henry Torac smiled.

Tony nodded vehemently. Jacob just looked down at his feet and grinned.

As if suddenly remembering his manners, Jacob said, "This is my friend Tony. We go to the same school."

"Good day to you, Tony." The old man shook Tony's hand. "And where do you fine boys attend school?"

Jacob didn't mind answering Musa Henry Torac's questions. He always asked gently, as though he cared.

"We go to George Jones Seminary for Boys. We leave tomorrow." Jacob's chest puffed out just a little. Even saying the name of his high school out loud made him feel proud.

"I have heard good things about that school ..."

"Come, old friend." Father appeared on the porch and smiled. "Everyone has arrived. We wait only for you."

Musa Henry Torac rubbed Jacob's head fondly and, with a nod to Tony, slowly climbed the steps into the house.

"He is very sad," said Tony.

"He is sad because his grandson was taken by Kony." Jacob spoke in a matter-of-fact voice. Tony's mouth dropped open. "They took him as he was walking home from school, and that is the last anyone has heard about him. He was just a little younger than us, then."

Jacob picked up his soda and took a big gulp. Kony was a madman, everyone said so. He was the leader of the Lord's Resistance Army, an army of abducted children.

"Did you know him? Musa Henry Torac's grandson, I mean?" asked Tony.

"No. He lived in Kitgum. But he was supposed to be very good in mathematics too. Father told me." Jacob shook his soda and watched the bubbles rise up the neck of the bottle.

Tony seemed to shrink down into his shirt. Jacob looked over at his friend and guessed what he was thinking.

"Kony cannot get *us*, you know. We are safe." Jacob knew something Tony didn't know. He had heard Father talking to Headmaster Heycoop about hiring extra guards to surround the school at night. There was no reason now to fear Kony and his rebel soldiers.

Should he tell Tony? Tony had no father; his family had no land. Jacob tried hard not to appear like a showoff, and the fact that his father knew the headmaster personally .... No, he wouldn't say anything about the extra guards.

"I will meet you at the bus tomorrow." Tony polished off his drink, set the bottle down, picked up his ball of rags, and dashed off. Tony never walked when he could run.

"It is time, Jacob." Ethel motioned with her hand. "Go and stand in the kitchen where your father can see you. He will call you when he is ready to talk. And when he is done with you, you must get ready to go with me to evening mass."

Most of the time Ethel was nice to Jacob, but not *nice–nice*, not like a mother is nice. His life would have been so different had his mother lived, Jacob thought. He closed his eyes and tried to see her face. Nothing. He was five when she died. *But dead is not dead. Spirits do not die. If they love you, they stay and protect you*, he thought.

Of course, if they died hating you, then they would plague you and make your life hard. A spirit could protect one person and hate another. But his mother loved him, and Jacob was sure that she would always protect him … even if he could not remember her.

Jacob tucked the ball under his arm and shuffled back into the house. Soon he would be back at school. He loved school. Not that he didn't like being home, because he did. And he loved the farm, too. Besides this house in Gulu, his father owned one of the biggest farms in Pader District, with thousands of cattle, goats, sheep, and pigs. And Father's cows were not just the common Ankole long-horned cattle, either. Father owned Jerseys and Friesians. That was why they were rich. A man's wealth was judged by how many cattle and how much land he owned.

"They will get you a fine wife one day." Father, rubbing Jacob's head and laughing, had said this himself as they had stood gazing at the herd just a few weeks ago.

Jacob walked down the hall, past the television room. When the generator was turned on, the channel was tuned to CNN from America or the BBC from England. But when Father was away, Ethel and Bella, the cook, along with whichever relatives might be visiting, huddled around the small box and watched the soap opera *Life's Like That* on Ugandan television. Jacob did not like the show. He couldn't keep the silly plots and characters straight in his head. Why watch the television when he could be playing football? He poked his head into the kitchen. Bella was preparing banana leaves for steaming. He could see her broad back and even broader behind. Bella was as big as a house, and she was old, maybe fifty. *Really* old.

Quietly, on tiptoes, Jacob crept through the kitchen measuring his footsteps to the *thwacks* of Bella's knife as she trimmed the leaves to fit the pot. If Bella noticed him she would pinch his cheeks and ask him stupid questions about school. Then she would say how much she would miss him. And *then* she would dab her eyes with her apron. Every time Jacob came home from school, Bella cried. Every time he returned to school, Bella cried. Bella's tears were annoying.

Once, he'd heard Bella say to Ethel that he would have a *sweet–sour* life because he was motherless. But his life was fine! Some children had lost their homes, and sometimes their families, and lived in the displacement camps. And think of the "night commuters." That's what people called the children who walked past their door every morning and evening, leaving the villages and camps because of their fear of a night raid by the Lord's Resistance Army. Imagine parents sending children on long, long walks away from their villages just to sleep in Gulu. His father would never do such a thing. The walk was hard on bare feet, and there was nothing to eat at the end of their journey. Now, *those* children had a *sour–sour* life. Really, Bella could be so infuriating.

Jacob sniffed. Roasted chicken, rolled and cooked in groundnuts—his favorite! On a far table, live grasshoppers popped and hummed in a pot, waiting their turn to be cooked. *Pop*, *pop*, *pop*—they banged against the lid of the pot in silly attempts to escape.

With his toes in the dust of the courtyard and his heels on the scarlet-red painted cement floor of the kitchen, Jacob tucked his football under him and sat down on it. Father and his guests sat under the dark green mango tree in the courtyard in high-backed cane chairs. Father, tall and fit, sat like a *kwaro*, a grandfather ready to tell tales of struggle and prosperity.

Quite suddenly, a loud, angry voice arose from the circle of men. The expression on Father's face changed abruptly from a smile to a grimace.

Okumu Adam, a well-travelled and educated man, slammed his fist down on the arm of his cane chair.

"What does President Museveni do about this Kony and his

army of children up here in the north? He is our president, the president of all of Uganda! He should send us more government soldiers. Our people need more protection."

"I will tell you," said another man, "Museveni does not want Kony caught because it gives him the excuse to keep such a big army." Jacob strained to see who was talking. It was Alwong Okumu, a teacher from the local university.

"No, no," the other guests protested. "Museveni may have taken over the presidency by force, but he has so far proven himself to be a good ruler. Think of the 1970s and General Idi Amin Dada's military rule. Thirty thousand murdered. My own brother killed!"

Jacob sighed. Why was it that men always talked politics?

Carefully, so Bella could not see, Jacob scooped a handful of groundnuts out of a bowl and, one by one, popped them into his mouth. As the voices of the men rose and fell, he gazed around. There were pots of black and red coffee beans in the corner. Twisty *okuru-ogwal* bushes climbed up the walls of the courtyard. If these were touched, even lightly, barbs would prick the skin and eventually painful blisters would erupt, spewing out pus in runny, yellow globs. And if the *okuru-ogwal* bushes did not deter thieves, jagged pieces of glass cemented into the ledge of the wall surely would.

The men in the courtyard fell silent as each in turn placed a straw in the pot of *lacoi* and took a long sip. The liquid was milky white, thick and potent.

And then Musa Henry Torac spoke, his ancient voice catching and cracking.

"Kony and his army rush out of the bush and cut off the feet of anyone caught riding a bicycle. This Kony is of the Acholi tribe, just like us, but he attacks mostly us. He must be caught. How could such an evil man continue to exist?"

Tears glistened in his eyes as he raised his fist in the air. His hand began to shake and rattle like a medicine man's *ajaa*. The arm fell and he covered his face with his hands.

"*Beast*," whispered Musa Henry Torac. "They call my grandson a beast." He slumped into his chair.

There was silence all around. To show such emotion was not the way of an Acholi man.

"My grandson's name is Michael, after Saint Michael, the warrior. Did not Saint Michael fight Satan in Heaven? Perhaps a child with such a name could fight Satan on earth? And is this Kony not Satan himself ?"

Musa Henry Torac looked up through the branches of the tree, up to the sky, as if the answer might be written on the clouds. To lose family was to lose all.

Jacob lifted his hand and dunked it into the bowl of groundnuts. Empty. He looked over at old Bella, or rather at Bella's big backside. He wasn't the least bit worried about Kony and his army. Not anymore. When he was little he'd had nightmares about being snatched away, but it was impossible to go on being scared all the time. After a while, Jacob just stopped worrying. Besides, Father would protect him. What he *was* worried about was Bella' discovering that he had eaten the whole bowl of nuts. He crouched down and made himself even smaller.

"What are you doing there?" Oh no, Bella had spotted him!

"What are you listening to, boy?"

She cocked her ear like a small dog toward a suspicious sound and heard the name "Kony." The corners of Bella's mouth turned down; her eyes narrowed.

"Man talk. Not for you." She waved her knife. "Go now. Find someone to play with." Bella's knife *swish-swished* in the air.

Jacob leapt to his feet and grimaced. He liked old Bella, maybe even loved her, but she would not stop treating him like a little kid. He opened his mouth to protest.

"Jacob, there you are." Father took long strides across the courtyard toward him. He looked elegant and powerful in his Western clothes. Father was a big man, and very strong, while Jacob took after his mother, small and slender with a thin nose and large eyes. Jacob straightened his shoulders and made himself tall, or as tall as possible.

"I will not see you again until the next school break, my son," said his father quietly. "I leave tonight for Kampala, and after that for London, England."

His mother's sing-song voice jumped into his head.

Pussycat, pussycat, where have you been?
I've been to London to visit the Queen.
Pussycat, pussycat, what did you there?
I frightened a little mouse under her chair.

Father had a brother in England. He had visited him many years before. On that visit he had brought home a book filled with silly poems that British children knew. The pictures were bright and funny—cats wearing boots and pink ladies in orange pumpkin shells.

"Is there anything I should bring you back from England?" asked his father.

Yes, yes! He almost leapt up and down. New CDs, comic books, a cellphone that took pictures? But to ask for such things would make him sound selfish, so instead Jacob said, "A football, please." It was a silly thing to ask for. He had one already.

"A football it is—the best in the Empire. I will be thinking of you. Do me proud this term, and do not forget your culture. You are with many tribes at school, and that is good, but you are Acholi. A person without culture is like a person without land. Work hard, my son."

His father gently rubbed his head in the way that Jacob loved, the way only his father ever did.

"I will, Father," he promised.

2
THE NIGHT COMMUTERS

"Jacob, come!" Ethel's voice rang out like an irritating gong. Jacob slipped his feet into sandals. He picked up the little blue Bible that he had won in a school debating contest, a wind-up flashlight to light his way home, and two five-thousand shilling notes for the church box. They were very old and very dirty and if he rubbed them hard enough between his thumb and fingers they might disintegrate entirely. Ethel tapped her foot impatiently.

If only she wouldn't make him go to church all the time. Really, Ethel went to church to pray for a husband and to talk to the *padi*, the priest. Priests could talk to the Big God. Ethel was a good Catholic, like Jacob and his parents. Ethel visited the medicine woman, too, but only on weekdays. Medicine men and women could appease the small gods. Ethel had told him so, and she had also explained that one must not visit the priest *and* the medicine men or women on the same day. That would cause a conflict between the gods.

Jacob did not *want* to believe in witchcraft. Witchcraft was old-fashioned, part of another time, not part of the new Uganda. Still, it would be wrong to show disrespect to the old gods of his tradition. After all, anything was possible. Except Ethel's finding a husband. That would never happen, Jacob was sure of it. She was too skinny and too bossy. And she was old—almost twenty-five.

Reluctantly, begrudgingly, he trailed Ethel out of the house and down the path. The church was on the opposite side of the city; it was a long way through the centre of town. Complaining was useless. Besides, by this time tomorrow he would be back at school.

His family lived in the "senior quarter" of Gulu, a residential area built by whites in the 1920s and '30s. Back then, his father said, the *munu* went to nightclubs, drank homemade alcohol, and played cricket and a card game called bridge. It was different now. Most of the *munu* in Gulu drove around in big Jeeps with names like AMREF, War Child, UNICEF, and World Health painted on the sides. These were organizations that helped the people of Uganda, although just *how* they helped was a mystery to Jacob.

Ethel scowled at the gun-toting watchman sitting in the little guard box by the front gate. Ethel said that paying the guard was a waste of money. "He would run away if he saw Kony coming down the road," she said. "It would be better if your father bought me a gun." Jacob thought that that was a good idea too. If anyone could fight off the LRA rebel soldiers, it was Ethel.

He took long, easy breaths of the cool evening air as he fell into step behind Ethel. The scent of shea nut oil wafted behind her, and whiffs of butter and sour milk. It wasn't a bad smell.

The buildings of Gulu were painted blue, yellow, and orange. Kiosks, shops, stalls, and wooden lean-tos were propped against crumbling buildings. Jacob loved his city. He navigated over the ruptured roads that ran through the town, with open sewers on either side. The black tarmac rose up in the heat, creating tiny volcano-like eruptions. Cars and trucks swerved around bumps and holes, making walking all the more precarious. Where the black, blistered hardtop ended, beaten, sandy roads began. The sand was soft under Jacob's feet.

And then he saw them … the night commuters. As they did every night, the children were coming from their displacement camps or villages to sleep on the streets of Gulu. They would be gone when the sun rose again. At first, Jacob had felt sorry for them. It was easy to feel badly for a few children. But now, they numbered in the thousands. There were just too many to feel sorry about.

"Jacob, you are too slow," Ethel turned back and called out. With a sigh, Jacob walked more quickly, jumping ahead of a night commuter, slowing down again the instant Ethel turned away.

"*Boda*," someone called out. "*Boda, boda*." A motorcycle-taxi came to an abrupt stop, kicking up a cloud of red dust. More dust in the teeth. Bananas sizzled on open grills alongside dried fish and papayas. Men, already drunk on *arege*, squatted on their haunches. There were wooden cases of bottled Coke and Krest for sale, and local orange soda, too. Jacob unfurled his fingers and looked down at the two notes in the palm of his hand. A Coke would cost only a few shillings …

"Jacob, hurry!" Again Ethel bellowed. Jacob sighed and ran a few steps, or pretended to. A truck honked, its tires spewing stones on all sides. A Jeep stopped in the road.

"Munu, mina cwit!" A group of children circled the Jeep. "White man, please, give me sweets!" The *munu* lowered his dark glasses and smiled as he rolled down his window and handed out hard candies wrapped in gold foil.

They had almost crossed the city of Gulu when a buzz raced like an electric current down the line of night commuters. Over and over, Jacob heard the words *Faster* and *Quickly* above the soft sound of bare feet slapping against the ground. Many tried to run, but most of the little ones were exhausted.

"Mak wot," one child hissed to another and another and

another. A big sister grabbed her little brother's hand. *"Oyot oyot,"* she pleaded when the boy reached down to pick up a broken rubber *sapatu.* "Hurry, hurry." They must claim their sleeping space for the night before Africa abruptly turned from gold to black. Even now, jagged fingers of red, orange, pink, and purple light curled into a fist as the sun dropped below the horizon.

By the time Jacob reached Holy Rosary Church, it was pitch-black. The last of the night commuters ran around him as if he were a rock in a stream. Dozens of children had already collected in the church's courtyard. In a frenzy of giggles and laughter, children plunked themselves down on the cement ground. Soon there was only a thin path leading from the iron gate to the church door. After mass, and after the churchgoers had carefully picked their way out of the church's courtyard, the gate would be bolted shut.

Impatiently, foot tapping, Ethel waited for Jacob at the side door of the church.

"Do you have money for the collection box?" Jacob showed her the two notes in his hand.

Satisfied, Ethel continued up the aisle to sit as close to the *padi* as possible.

Jacob looked back at the children sleeping on the ground. At least *they* were not bossed around all the time. He poked his head into the church. The white fluorescent lights were almost blinding. If he sat near the open door maybe he would hear the night commuters talking. Sometimes there was a teacher or a storyteller among the children.

Lowering himself down to one knee, Jacob crossed himself and then slipped into a pew. At the very front of the church, Ethel knelt at the end of the long pew and then inched down the bench until she was directly in front of the *padi.* She immediately gazed up at the priest, all dewy-eyed. Jacob knew the look.

The new *padi* was young and white—pink, really—with startling grey hair that grew out of startling places—his nose and ears mostly. He had been sent out from Rome months ago and had yet to adjust to the light, the dark, or the heat. Even now he looked as if he might melt into his shoes.

Priests were curious things. Just after his mother's death, the old priest had told Jacob that God had taken his mother to live with Him and that she was happy now. Jacob thought that she had been happy being alive. The priest seemed to know what he was thinking. He told Jacob that he must not question the wisdom of God, then gave him a toffee.

He was so bored. *452 times 8 equals 3,616.* Too easy. *96 times 75 equals 7,200.* Still too easy. He'd have to practise more if he wanted to win the multiplication contest at school this year. *678 times 67 equals 45,423.* No, the answer had to end in an even number: *45,426.* The winner got to go to Kampala to compete in the national finals.

"Amen," sang the congregation.

His eyes drifted up. Above, black baby angels wearing white robes and white fluffy wings were painted on the ceiling of the church. They looked trapped. When he was little, he had given them names.

He looked to the side and saw a tall boy sitting down the pew. The boy wore no shoes and his clothes were rags. He was a night commuter. His shoulders were pulled back and he held his head high. Still, there was a sadness to him, even Jacob could see that. Maybe he was hungry. Jacob unfurled his fingers and looked at the money in his hand. The deacon, in a white robe tied with a gold cord, spotted the boy too. He began to walk toward the boy. What if he asked him to leave? That would not be fair. Jacob slid over. "Hello," whispered Jacob.

The deacon paused. He recognized Jacob. Jacob's father was a great financial supporter of the church. The deacon turned away and carried on with his duties.

The night commuter turned. The boy's eyes were almond shaped, his nose and cheekbones sculpted into ridges, his mouth wide, as if designed to smile.

"Are you …" Jacob paused. He did not want to insult the boy. "Are you hungry?"

"I am not a beggar," said the boy quietly and with dignity.

"I know. I …" Jacob's eyes darted around the church. Ethel had her head bowed in prayer, the priest had his eyes closed, and the deacon now had his back to the congregation. Ethel would be so angry if she knew what he was about to do. Jacob slipped the two five-thousand shilling notes for the collection box into the boy's palm. The boy's eyes grew round with astonishment.

"Take it and go," Jacob's whisper turned into a hiss. If Ethel caught him he'd be in trouble forever.

"Thank you." The boy rose to leave. "What is your name?" Jacob whispered.

The boy stopped and stared. It was a funny question for a rich boy to ask a boy like him, and Jacob himself was amazed that he had said it.

"Oteka, my name is Oteka." The boy's fingers curled tightly around the notes.

"My name is Jacob."

Oteka's eyes warmed with thanks. "Where do you come from?" Jacob asked. "The camp," he whispered.

Again the deacon began walking toward them. Oteka caught sight of him, then moved swiftly, like a panther or maybe a lion, and vanished into the night. He left the door to the courtyard ajar.

"It's an old story told in many countries ..."

A storyteller! As Jacob's ears caught the words drifting in from the courtyard, his eyes searched out Ethel. She was kneeling now, her head bent in prayer.

"A scorpion came up to a crocodile as it bathed in mud at the edge of Prince Albert Lake."

The priest spoke. "I believe in God the Father Almighty ..."

"The scorpion said, 'Crocodile, take me across the lake.' Surprised and perplexed, the crocodile said, 'Why should I? You will just sting me and I will die.' And to that the scorpion replied, 'If I sting you while we are out in the water then we will both die because I cannot swim.'"

Jacob teetered on the edge of the pew, one ear cocked toward the voice of the storyteller, the other trying to block out the hum of prayers.

"Maker of Heaven and earth ..."

"The crocodile agreed to take the scorpion across the lake. Now, halfway across the great lake of Prince Albert the scorpion did exactly what he had said he would not do. He stung the crocodile. Imagine the old crocodile's shock and astonishment! As the crocodile began to sink, he cried out, 'But you will die too! Why did you do that?'

"'Because,' said the scorpion ..."

The deacon slammed the church door shut.

"No!" Jacob leapt up. What was the end of the story? Why did the scorpion kill the crocodile and himself in the bargain?

The deacon gave him a hard stare. He sat down with a thump. The priest finished the prayer.

"Amen," sighed Jacob.

3
OTEKA

The limbs of the night commuters were stiff and the chill from the ground had to be shaken from their bones. But as soon as their eyes opened, the children were up and walking.

Oteka, especially, had good reason to leave Gulu quickly and walk the ten kilometers back to the camp where he now lived. The medicine man had said that it would cost one hundred thousand shillings to have his question answered. The two five-thousand shilling notes that were folded tightly in his hand, added to the ninety thousand shillings he had hidden in his hut, would at last be enough. Begging, selling, working—it had taken him almost a year to collect this princely sum.

Pink-headed and pink-tailed lizards skittered back and forth across the dusty road. Oteka paid them no mind as his walk turned into a jog and then into a slow run. The morning sun turned the air a buttery yellow and the red road underfoot was dry. Soon the rains would come and the road would become a ruby river.

Every kilometer or so the white man's *mutoka* honked, and Oteka had to pitch himself into the tall grass by the roadside to avoid being hit. These Jeeps carried the *munu* to and from the Murchison Falls game reserve a hundred kilometres down this same road. Hippos and crocodiles, lions and leopards, giraffes and birds of all sorts lived on the reserve. Oteka knew all about the park. His grandfather had been a guide to white hunters many years ago, when it was still possible to hunt great game. Oteka would have liked to see a lion—just once.

The hum of the camp was welcoming as he approached—a morning song of blended voices, of women greeting the day and each other, of roosters crowing and babies wailing.

"Oteka, Oteka." An old woman sitting on a *kolo* outside her mud and cow-dung hut called to him.

Oteka crouched down and smiled into the old woman's milky eyes. "Adaa, I am back." It might have been a silly thing to say—after all, he was right in front of her—but Adaa's eyesight was failing. Besides, it was their custom to greet each other this way. Oteka had no family and Adaa had no family, so they had become each other's family—the fifteen-year-old boy and the seventy-year-old woman.

"What happened to your family?" Oteka had once asked Adaa the question, but she could not respond. She could not speak the names of her son and his family for fear of crying. So it was another woman, an old friend of Adaa's from the same village, who had shared Adaa's story with him.

Adaa had once lived with her son, her daughter-in-law, and their three children on a small farm. To see a son well married and prosperous and her grandchildren strong and healthy—it was a good life. Adaa was a gifted weaver and could support herself and take care of her grandchildren while her daughter-in-law tended the garden. They grew maize, cassava, and vegetables of all kinds. Her son took care of the chickens, pigs, and goats, and they had enough money to send the two oldest boys to school. Such blessings she had!

"Many in the village envied her," said Adaa's old friend. "Perhaps someone put a curse on her, someone who was jealous, because one night the LRA descended. There was screaming, and rounds of bullets made silver streaks in the night sky. There were long, sharp knives too." The old friend paused. "We heard the screams. Later, it was said that Adaa's son and daughter-in-law fought off the LRA with their bare hands while Adaa sheltered the children with her body. The screaming stopped suddenly, and Adaa was cast aside like rubbish, not even worthy of killing. All three children were taken by the LRA, along with the goats, the chickens, the food stored up for the rainy season. Everything—gone. Adaa was left alone with her dead son and daughter-in-law."

The story made Oteka shake with anger, and he had promised himself right then and there that he would not leave her. How could he, when she reminded him so much of his own grandmother?

Oteka, too, remembered what happiness felt like, what it meant to be safe, to have a future, to have a family.

"You will go to the university and become a doctor." His father would repeat these words often as he rubbed his son's head.

"Perhaps I will drive a truck like you," suggested Oteka.

"That may be," nodded Father. "We do share a gift, my son. We always know the right path to take." On a continent with few road signs, having a keen sense of direction was a true blessing. "And you will play football!" Father threw up his hands and laughed. His father was very smart, spoke five languages, and drove trucks for a big company in Kampala. The money was good, but it took him away from home for weeks—sometimes months—on end.

Oteka's mother was tall and slim and could read and write. She did not hit her children, which caused the neighbors to say that her children would misbehave and grow up crooked. They were a small family, just Oteka, the oldest, Ocira, only four years old, and baby Esther. They had four cows, a goat, a dozen hens, and one rooster, which crowed mid-afternoon and sometimes in the middle of the night. Once, after having been woken from sleep once too often, Mother went after the rooster with a knife. She chased him around and around. He was old but slippery. Oteka begged his mother to spare the old rooster, but it was hard to beg and laugh at the same time! In the end, the rooster lived to wake them up another night.

Their farm was a tropical garden of banana, mango, palm, and tamarind trees, and coffee trees too. Oteka loved it best when the flowers on the coffee trees were in bloom and cool air blew through their leaves. The grass was long, and the stream that ran through their farm was clean. Collecting the water from the village well was his job. Even as a very small boy, Oteka hauled two buckets every day, one for washing and the other for cooking. Water was used sparingly.

They ate twice a day, although, like everyone else in the village, only once a day during the dry season. Oteka went to school. He had many friends. He had sandals. They lived in paradise.

Then one day his father came home from his travels a sick man. His sickness was called *twoo jonyo*, or *kisipi,* or *cilim,* the slimming disease. It had many names. A white nurse who came to the village to give needles called his father's disease AIDS. She was not kind or sympathetic. After a few months, Father's eyes began to bulge, his cheekbones stood out, and diarrhea ran down his legs like brown water dribbling out of a rusted pipe. Father went to the foreign doctors for a cure. When they had none, Mother called in the medicine man.

Father disapproved of witchcraft. "I have been to many countries in my truck—to Botswana, Somalia, Rwanda, and South Africa, and all the places in between. Witchcraft is false. Accept the Christian God and His stone saints as the Big God," said his father. The whole family walked to church twice a week. It was far away and it took hours to reach it. Mother was Catholic too, and so she went to the medicine man only when the Big God did not help, only when necessary. When Father became too sick to walk to church, she felt that it was necessary.

The medicine man came and used his *jogi* and spear to find the poison around the home but Father did not get well.

A second medicine man said that the house was cursed and many hens, goats, and even a cow had to be sacrificed. A third medicine man said that a *lajok,* a witch doctor with great and evil powers, had put a curse on Father for having four cows, a goat, and chickens. Mother sold the cows and the goat and used much of the money to pay for the medicine men. Then she walked the many kilometres to church almost every day and put more notes and coins into the box. She prayed to the Big God until her knees, her legs, and her back were so stiff and sore it was hard to stand.

One day an auntie came and offered to care for the children. She looked each child up and down through narrow, nut-hard eyes. Oteka was too big she said, and baby Esther was too small. She picked Ocira. Auntie lived near the Sudanese border. The Lord's Resistance Army was near. It was dangerous but Auntie said not to worry about abduction, it was better Ocira lived away from *twoo jonyo* AIDS. Auntie took Ocira's hand and left. Mother cried, "Soon, soon we will be together again."

Father died. The priest would not come to give him funeral rites. He had a big Jeep but said that travelling to their village was too dangerous. The LRA were in the area. The men of their village would not bury his father. "Don't touch, don't touch, the disease might spread," they whispered one to another. Never mind that tradition told them that those who denied anyone a proper burial would be haunted until the day they too died. Never mind that those who shirked their duty risked offending the gods.

An uncle took pity on Oteka and, using a dry wooden pole, pushed the body of his father into the grave. Dry wood, he said, would not transmit the disease. His father's body was wrapped up in a gunnysack. There was a thud and a gust of dust as his father's body fell into the hole.

"Father," Oteka whispered above his grave, "Forgive me." Then Oteka hid behind their hut and cried.

His father was buried in a field far away. The elders of the village decided that Father's grave could not be near their huts, where the disease could worm its way up through the soil. Without his father's grave nearby, Oteka would not feel his father's fortifying presence and would not benefit from his father's goodwill and strength.

When Oteka's baby sister, Esther, died of *twoo jonyo* AIDS, Oteka alone buried her.

As his beautiful mother grew weaker and weaker it was Oteka who bathed her and dripped water onto her parched tongue. People remarked, "He has a strong spirit." They admired him, but they would not go near him or his mother.

Then a man from Auntie's village arrived. He said that four-year-old Ocira had died of malaria. The news left Oteka breathless. "Ocira, Ocira, my brother," he cried. But Oteka had no time to think, no time to grieve.

When dirt fell over his mother's wasted body, he pleaded with any god who would listen, big or small, "Do not leave me here alone. Take me too." But he was strong, and so he lived.

Oteka stayed with his grandmother until he was fourteen years old, but then a year ago, before the rains, she too had died.

And so Oteka and Adaa adopted one another, with each doing what they could for the other. Adaa was too old and now too blind to do the cooking, although she prepared the vegetables. Oteka did the grinding of the corn and most of the cooking. The other boys laughed at him for doing "woman's work" but he shrugged them off.

Oteka cooked cassava and sweet potatoes, steamed maize and *do-do* harvested from the garden. Sometimes they ate pumpkin mixed with shelled groundnuts, but mostly they ate cassava. Other times they ate the mush the people from the United Nations doled out in great, bleached bags with blue stripes down the side. Occasionally the women in the camp took pity and invited them to share in a tasty meal of rat, boiled, rolled in nuts, and baked over an open fire. In return, Oteka became an expert at preparing chickens to cook: a chop to the neck to kill them, drain the blood, dip the chicken in boiling water, pluck it while still warm, remove the giblets.

Despite all his skill in finding and preparing food, Oteka was always hungry. But his belly was not bloated, and the tips of his hair had not turned to rust—these were sure signs of malnutrition. He was healthy enough. But daily life, the gardening, preparing the food, the cooking, it took time—time not spent learning, time not spent in school. He would not be a doctor as his father had hoped. "I have enough money now, Adaa." Oteka grinned as he held out his hand to show her the notes.

"It is good that you now have what you need."

She smiled. Not for the first time, Adaa gazed at the boy through foggy eyes and admired him. He was a tall boy, so good looking. He reminded her of her own son, and that thought caused her as much pain as happiness. "Sit for a moment." Adaa patted the ground in front of her.

Oteka took in a breath. As much as he cared for her, he had no time to listen to an old woman's ramblings. Still, out of respect, he sat.

"All Acholi names have meanings, this you know. Do you know the meaning of the name your parents gave you?" Adaa's old eyes narrowed.

"It means *hero*." Oteka stared at the ground. He was embarrassed. He was no hero.

"That is true. It also means *victory*. I can tell by the name they gave you that your parents had great hopes for you. And so do I. Soon you will be off in search of your own path."

"I will not leave you here, Adaa." Oteka made the promise and meant it.

"Soon I will join my family in the world beyond reach. But listen carefully, Oteka. When I am in the world that cannot be touched, I will reach back and protect you with all my might. You see me now as old and weak, but inside I am young and strong. That is how it is with all people, no matter where they live, no matter where they come from. Now I ask you, do you believe in the medicine man, my son?"

Oteka nodded his head, but not vigorously, not with commitment.

The old woman paused, then reached out and gently ran her withered hands over his arms.

"You see these arms? They are strong—strong like the limbs of the great *owii* tree. Why have you reached such a height? Surely you are this tall and straight so that you may one day touch the clouds. But to be tall and rigid means that you may one day break. Like the great *owii* tree, you too must learn to bend and sway in the wind. And look at these arms. One day these strong arms will turn into wings and take you up to the Big God. And see these feet, look how they carry you. Look how swift you are, how powerful. Like the roots of the mighty *owii* tree, these feet are your roots, and your roots are your culture, and your culture is witchcraft. Go, my son, go and ask the medicine man your question."

The old woman smiled as he leapt up and charged into his own hut, ducking his head but still clipping the straw that hung down from the thatched roof.

Oteka's mud hut was cool and welcoming. A place was carved out for everything he owned. There was a rag ball made of plastic garbage bags and bits of twine, and a second shirt from the UN charity bags with the words *Mont Tremblant* embossed on the pocket. He had a scratchy blanket with *UN* stamped on the top and an old towel with the words *Lion King* sprawled across it.

Oteka flipped back the mat on the floor, then dug up a metal box hidden in a hole. It had belonged to his mother. He counted out the ninety thousand shillings and added the new ten thousand shillings he would use to buy a white hen. The medicine man might yet ask for a sheep, or even a goat, which made him nervous. Oteka could afford neither.

"I'll be back, Adaa." Oteka laughed as he ran past her. The old woman lifted a heavy hand, smiled, then looked up at the sun and wondered why it had grown so dark so early in the day.

It took less than ten minutes to negotiate with a farmer for the white hen. It took another ten minutes to race across the camp. Thousands now lived in the displacement camp. Many families starved, yet they could see their farms from this distance, their very own land and homes. And yet lurking about, often between them and their land, was Kony and his band of child soldiers.

Oteka ran past the bamboo shower stalls and communal kitchens. The smell of cooking palm oil was in the air. He raced past the women pounding cassava into flour and around an old storyteller who was welcoming home straggling night commuters. Even now, tired from their walk and with no food in their bellies, the older children were rushing to the schoolroom run by the United Nations. The women were off tending to the gardens. Young and old men were setting up chessboards, some on spindly tables, others on mats on the ground. In the distance he could see the hospital, a stark, cement building that harboured a dozen iron beds, paper-thin mattresses, and a lone medical assistant in a white lab coat. Beside it, and down a small hill, were the latrines.

Out of breath, Oteka came to a sudden stop several metres away from the medicine man's hut. He calmed himself, inhaled deeply, and walked toward the medicine man with all due reverence and respect.

The medicine man—a man of fifty years or more with a shrivelled belly and tangled hair and six teeth (three up and three down)—sat cross-legged on a mat in front of his hut. Life in the camp had reduced his weight and his fortunes considerably, but still he sat with a regal bearing and surveyed the world around him. As Oteka approached, the medicine man took note of the white hen as he looked Oteka up and down.

"Medicine man." Oteka bowed respectfully. "I need to talk to my mother."

4
MEDICINE MAN

"Do you have the money?" The medicine man's piercing eyes made Oteka squirm.

Oteka laid the notes, and a few coins too, out on the mat.

The medicine man nodded. In better times he would have considered such a sum beneath him but now … it was enough.

"I see the white hen, but what of the goat or sheep? The small gods must be appeased."

"This is all I have." Oteka bowed again. His heart began to pound. To save the money to buy a sheep or a goat would take a long time, too long.

"And what of your father, your brothers, sisters, and cousins? Can they not help you?"

"I am alone." Oteka looked at the ground. He was ashamed.

"Then I ask you, do you believe?" "Yes." The word came out in a whisper.

Did he? He was a Christian. But if there was a chance, even a small one, then surely the Big God would understand. And besides, did not the Big God create everything? He must have created the medicine man, too. And might the Big God speak through one of His own creations? Such was Oteka's reasoning.

After scratching various parts of his body, pondering, considering, and raising his eyes to the heavens, the medicine man nodded. "I cannot guarantee that the small gods will help with such a humble sacrifice, but they may take pity on a boy who has no family. It depends—the gods can be stubborn. But," the medicine man held up one spindly finger, "we can try. Wait here."

Oteka leapt into the air with gratitude.

The medicine man's first and second wives had already left to work in the gardens. It was the third, youngest wife who would assist. She was only a few years older than Oteka but seemed sure of her duties. With a careless wave she plucked the squawking chicken out of his arms and tossed it into the hut.

The medicine man stood, stretched, and without saying another word ducked his head and disappeared into the gloom of his mud hut. With his eyes following the medicine man, Oteka didn't notice the young wife coming up behind him. Striking like a cobra she snatched a clump of Oteka's hair and yanked it out by the roots. Before he had time to protest, she reached down, grabbed his hand, and peeled off a bit of his nail. Oteka remained mute and unmoved. He felt no pain. The magic had started.

"Sit."

Oteka sat. The sun was climbing in the sky and he felt beads of sweat gather on his brow. Incense wafted out of the hut, and the rattle of the *ajaa* bells bade the smaller gods come visit. When the sun was almost overhead, the young wife emerged from the hut and nodded. The medicine man was ready.

Oteka's heart began to thump. He entered the hut.

It was a dim and shadowy place. Wild animal skins lined the walls—antelope and lion, and the most treasured of all, the skin of a leopard. Mats covered the dirt floor. Crossed spears and drums were to the left of the mat. A candle provided the only light.

"Sit," commanded the young wife.

Cross-legged, with watering eyes, Oteka sat. His thumping heart was now pounding in his ears, his palms were wet with sweat. The medicine man—now wearing beads, skins, and *gagi* around his ankles and wrists, with ash and paint on his forehead and chest—began his duty. He took a sip of holy water, then spat it out. He shook the *gagi* to invite the spirits in. The young wife lit more incense. The smoke stung Oteka's eyes.

"Why have you come here?" the medicine man shouted as he rattled the shells and beads and pounded on the drum.

"My mother." Oteka could barely form words. "I must speak with her."

The medicine man roared and danced and called to the gods to make their presence known. And then, when he seemed depleted, he hissed to his young wife, "Bring me the chicken. The gods are being stubborn today."

The young wife knelt beside the medicine man and held the chicken up to him in an offering. The medicine man grabbed the screeching chicken by the neck, then pried open its beak.

"Spit in the mouth of the chicken," commanded the medicine man. Oteka did as he was told. Then the medicine man did the same. The fingernail clipping and hair that the wife had taken from Oteka were mixed with herbs and that concoction, too, was shoved down the chicken's throat.

Again the medicine man shook his beads and shells, but now he stood, and the roof of the hut seemed to rise to accommodate his height. The smoke grew thicker, encasing Oteka in a fog. It was nearly impossible for him to keep his eyes open longer than a few seconds. As the medicine man's hands reached up and up and up, as his voice vibrated with chants that rose from rumbles to thunder claps, the sounds engulfed then swamped Oteka. Then, in one broad sweep, the medicine man wrenched a knife from his belt and, with a mighty swipe, he severed the chicken's head.

"Ask your question." The medicine man's voice was low and gritty, like a rake being dragged over rocky ground.

"Mother," Oteka whispered. "I do not know where I am or where I am supposed to be in this life. I wait here in the camp only for my grave. Tell me, what must I do? Please, Mother, tell me."

The medicine man held the chicken high and swung it by the neck, all the while howling, "Here is your boy, Mother. You have heard him speak. He needs your help. He is stranded in this time but he can escape his situation. I am a medium and I beg you to speak to your child. LET HIM HEAR YOUR VOICE. GIVE HIM A MESSAGE." The howl turned into a shriek and the candle was snuffed out.

Silence.

And then, "Kony." The word dripped out of the medicine man's mouth like poison. In that moment, Oteka felt more alone than ever.

Oteka reeled out of the medicine man's hut and staggered back across the camp. Reaching out, he took hold of a bamboo pole and tried to steady himself. He'd have retched if he'd had any food in his stomach. He came to the public showers, ducked his head inside, and pulled down on the chain of the cistern. Out dribbled a thin stream of water warmed by the sun.

Kony, the madman who stole, tortured, and murdered children. Was his mother trying to warn him? Should he run? But what if he was captured on the road? If he stayed, would he be caught in a raid? What was he to do? He wanted to cry out. If there was no escape, why torture him like this? Then another thought, a more rational one. Did he hear right or did he hear his own fears echoed back to him?

With great effort he walked back toward his hut, his feet dragging in the dust. What difference did it make?

He could not leave Adaa. There were many in the camp, thousands, who were starving. It was not like the old days in the villages, when neighbor cared for neighbor. What little resources each had went to their own children, their own survival. If Oteka left Adaa, she would surely starve. The answer was in that—to stay and fulfill his obligation to the old woman and wait for a sign.

"Adaa." Oteka neared the old woman's hut. The *kolo* in front was empty. Long white tubes of cassava sat in a bowl. Oteka looked about. The camp was quiet. Small children were sleeping, men played their chess games, and the girls and women had yet to return from the gardens.

"Adaa?"

Oteka pushed aside a strip of canvas that served as her door. In the dim light he saw the fish that hung from the roof, fish he had caught and Adaa had dried. He smelled beans and sesame. And then in the shadows he saw her.

"Oh, Adaa." Oteka fell onto his hands and knees and crawled, hand over hand, across the mud floor. He reached Adaa's *kabutu*, then gathered the little woman in his arms.

She had left this world peacefully. It was the sign.

5
SCHOOL DAYS

Ethel watched from the doorway as Jacob packed his tin suitcase.

"Do you need help?"

Jacob shook his head. He had been packing his own suitcase since he was six years old.

"Here. You take this." Ethel dropped a small bag of herbs into his bag. "This is for a sore throat. You get them too much."

Jacob grimaced. Ethel's potions and concoctions smelled like monkey dung and tasted even worse.

Beside his small aluminum case were two stacks of supplies. In one pile there was a change of clothes, his good shoes, pens, paper, notebooks, and two textbooks Father had ordered from Kampala. In the second pile there was a towel, two bars of soap (one for washing himself and the big blue bar for washing clothes), a sheet, a blanket, a bucket to haul water, and a torch. All but the bucket were packed neatly into the case. His mattress was standing near the door and had already been wound up tight with a cord. Jacob stood the bucket beside the mattress.

"And this is from Bella." Ethel handed him a *pekke.* Jacob tucked it into his case. The *pekke* contained a jar of peanut butter, some ketchup to make the school food edible, and biscuits.

"This is from me too." She handed him a small jar of sugar. "Now hurry, hurry. I will walk with you to the bus station," announced Ethel. She was always in a rush.

Once outside the house, Ethel swept up the suitcase, planted it on her head and, in long, even strides, swept out of the compound. Jacob tucked the rolled mattress under his arm, picked up the bucket in his other hand, and followed.

Small children gathered around a termite hill taller than he was. They poked strands of hay into the holes. Alive, fried, or even dipped in curry paste, white ants were tasty treats. Jacob stopped under a jacaranda tree to remove a pebble from his sandal. When in bloom the tree would be covered with purple flowers with a sweet smell. He shoved his sandal back on, then had to march double-time to catch up with Ethel.

The bus looked more like a beast than a machine. It carted forty or so passengers, plus assorted livestock, to the city limits and beyond. The whole back end of it sagged.

Where was Tony? No matter, the bus would not leave until the driver had enough occupants to make it worth his while, and so far it was only half full.

The bus driver revved the engine, then hollered to those walking by, "Come now, please, I am about to leave." When that didn't seem to work, the driver yelled out the door, "If you want home, come now." Still no takers. Finally the driver thumped down on his seat and cranked the radio up when a Bob Marley song came on. He waited.

Jacob's suitcase and mattress were tossed onto the roof of the bus. He kept the bucket with him. There were many seats left inside but he chose the one behind a goat, because there would be plenty of room on one side for Tony. He stretched over a fat granny and looked out the window.

"You will be a good boy this term and make your father proud!" Ethel hollered at him. She always said that. She'd even said it when he was six and going off to school for the very first time. Jacob nodded. He *would* be good, and he *would* make his father proud. Then he saw someone running.

"Tony!" Jacob bellowed. "Tony!"

With his mattress on his head and a bucket in his hand stuffed to the top with what little he had, Tony came jogging down the dusty road. Jacob waved frantically.

Tony did not have a silver tin suitcase like the other boys. His family could not afford to send him to school. But the nuns in his elementary school believed in him because he was smart and a good boy. They filled out many scholarship application forms. Finally, Tony was allowed to sit the entrance exam to George Jones Seminary for Boys.

Tony had told Jacob the story. "The nuns prayed and prayed. They told me that if I failed it was because I was an ungrateful boy, but if I passed it was God's work. Then they said that if I got into high school I should repay God by becoming a priest." At this part of the story Tony always laughed. He had never actually said it to his friends, but everyone knew that Tony really *wanted* to become a priest.

"I made it!" Beaming, his smile stretching from ear to ear, Tony boarded the bus, mattress and all. The goat nudged Jacob and looked at Tony's mattress with interest.

Ethel banged her fist against the side of the bus and said goodbye. Jacob leaned across the granny, waved out the open window, then made himself comfy.

Three more people climbed on the bus and there were greetings all around. Finally, with what sounded like a small explosion, the bus was launched and headed off down the bumpy road, to great cheers and claps.

The small city of Gulu was soon left behind. It was too noisy to talk, so the best he and Tony could do was to yell out to each other occasionally or to sing along with the radio.

A rutty, sandy, potholed road cut a swath through the countryside. Elephant grass, bush, and farmers' fields were all the eye could see. Soon they would meet up with their friend Paul. Jacob couldn't wait to hear the stories Paul would have to tell!

Paul was the biggest of the three boys, the best looking, and the bossiest. He spoke English and French, plus Acholi and Langi, of course. Though his family lived in Uganda's capital city, Kampala, Paul attended school with Jacob and Tony in northern Uganda because that was where his mother was from. Besides, the schools in the country were cheaper than the schools in the big city, *much* cheaper. Paul's father worked for an agency that was trying to provide people with clean drinking water. Paul's family did not own land. He was paid for his work, but everyone knew that money was nothing but dust in the mouth.

During the school break, Paul's father had gone to America to give a speech about the water quality in Uganda. The people Paul's father worked for said he could take his son, too. The white people in the office gave him something called "airline points," which meant that Paul could get a plane ticket to New York City. It was as close to a miracle as Paul ever expected to get!

The best part about Paul, in Jacob's opinion, was that even though he was from the great city of Kampala he didn't treat Jacob and Tony like villagers. He didn't laugh at them. Just the opposite. When Tony had first come to the school he'd tried to turn off a light bulb by touching it and burned his hand. When the other boys laughed at him, Paul threatened to knock all their heads off. They stopped laughing.

Two hours later the bus came to a grinding stop in front of the blue-and-white sign that read "George Jones Seminary for Boys." The school wasn't just a seminary, of course. Boys who did not plan to become Catholic priests went to the school as well—it was a good place for any boy to get an education.

"Come on!" Jacob grabbed his bucket, pushed the goat aside, said goodbye to the granny, and the two boys scrambled off the bus.

"This one?" A man standing on the roof of the bus held up a mattress roll.

"Yes, please and thank you," Jacob yelled back. His mattress roll and tin suitcase came hurtling off the roof, landing with a thud and a cough of dust. They turned and ran through the gates of the George Jones Seminary for Boys.

6
AMERICA AND BULL'S BLOOD

Young guards sporting small guns with wooden handles stood watching the boys enter the school. Were these the extra guards his father had asked for? They looked bored, or maybe angry. Certainly they did not look as though they would or could fight off the LRA. One guard in particular glared at the boys with loathing. Jacob understood why. The students at George Jones Seminary for Boys were special, lucky. They would have an education, feed their children, have a *sweet–sweeter* life.

Once through the gates they saw the familiar square of green grass with a sprawling mango tree planted in the middle. Classes were held under the tree, and students often ate under it, too. The grass had been trimmed that very morning. Women from a nearby displacement camp would come often with babies on their backs and cut the grass with long slashers.

To Jacob's eye, everything looked welcoming. The white-and-turquoise stucco chapel, which was also the assembly hall, was directly ahead. Classrooms in red-brick buildings with big, airy windows were to the left, and a large, one-storey building housing three dormitories sat to the right of the open square.

Shouts and welcomes greeted them. The air was filled with names and cheers. On the first day of school everyone was a friend.

"What took you?" Paul, as large and gangly as a baby zebra,

came out of nowhere and tackled Jacob to the ground. Tony flung aside his mattress and bucket, took a giant leap into the air, and pitched himself on top.

"Get off! Get off !"

When they eventually rolled off him, Jacob lay flat out, his whole body convulsing with laughter. He looked up at the sky. School felt like home. Jacob's grin spread from ear to ear as he crawled back up onto his feet.

"Catch." Paul flung Jacob's mattress at him. He caught it and fell down again.

"BOYS! Enough!" Mr. Otim, the assistant headmaster, took long strides toward them. Dressed in a Western-style blue suit, white shirt, and striped tie, he gave each boy a hard stare. Mr. Otim could throw a sour face across open ground like an Olympic athlete could throw a javelin.

Paul reached down and yanked Jacob to his feet. Tony banged his head into Paul's butt, then fell back into the dirt. Paul and Jacob nearly exploded with laughter. Mr. Otim just rolled his eyes and walked away.

"Hurry. I've already picked out your beds. You have to unpack before prayers." Paul hoisted Jacob's suitcase onto his shoulder, Jacob and Tony picked up their mattresses and buckets, and the boys raced each other all the way to the dorm.

There were three dorm rooms at their school. The dormitory building was shaped like a T. All three dorms were connected by a common room at the top of the T. In each of the three rooms, a long line of brown-painted iron beds greeted the students, twenty cots on each side, forty beds to a room.

Jacob, Paul, and Tony had been assigned to dorm room number one. The cot Paul had picked out for Jacob was the third on the right, the one closest to the door.

"Tony, you are in bed number five." He pointed to a spring cot. Paul had cot number four. He liked being in the middle of things.

Paul hurled himself onto Jacob's bedsprings and bounced up and down, for no reason whatsoever, making a rackety creaking noise.

"Off!" Jacob grabbed Paul's arms, hauled him off the bedsprings, then rolled out his thin mattress.

"Ah, there you are. I have been waiting to talk to you three."

It was Mr. Ojok, their don. He also taught chemistry, mathematics, and algebra, Jacob's best subjects. He had even studied in England. Everyone thought he was a very good teacher.

"We have a new boy, Okello Norman." Mr. Ojok spoke in what Jacob thought of as his "teacher voice." "He's younger than the rest of you, only twelve, but he has excelled in all his classes. He is here on a full mathematic scholarship. Given your interest in mathematics, Jacob, I thought you might make him feel welcome."

Mathematics? Jacob frowned. The boy must be good to have won such a scholarship. But *how* good? Imagine losing the mathematics prize this year to a twelve-year-old!

"Jacob, are you paying attention?" Jacob's head snapped up. "Yes, sir."

"Good, because I want all three of you to be responsible for him. See that his first few weeks go smoothly."

Three hearts plummeted. That's all they needed—to care for a brainy *ongee.* And one who would probably cry himself to sleep, too. As long as he didn't wet the bed. There was no protecting a bed-wetter.

"Do I make myself clear?" Mr. Ojok repeated.

Jacob's, Tony's, and Paul's heads bobbed against their chests.

"Look up. May I have your word? Each of you?"

"Yes, sir." All three boys straightened up and nodded smartly.

Mr. Ojok looked down at the clipboard in his hand. "There are thirty-eight boys in this dorm. Two more will be joining us in a few days. See that all the new boys are made welcome." And with that, he bustled away, all business.

"Have you met Norman?" Jacob dumped his clothes and shoes in the footlocker at the end of the bed. Tony didn't have much to unpack—a pair of shoes from the UN bag, an extra shirt, and some school supplies given to him by the nuns.

"No, but I have seen him. *Otidi*." Paul put his hand mid-chest. Jacob rolled his eyes. Not only was Norman twelve years old, but he was a *short* twelve-year-old.

"That's his bed." Paul pointed to a bed across from Jacob's. "But never mind him, we'll be late for prayers if you don't hurry."

Paul pressed his face against the iron bars on the windows. The bars had been installed last term to prevent anyone from climbing in. "As a precaution," Mr. Ojok had told them all, adding, "You boys are perfectly safe here."

Paul looked past the mango tree and across the grass to the far building. A line of students had already begun filing into the chapel. The prefects could cane a boy for being late for prayers, or worse, dispatch him to the kitchen to peel heaps of potatoes. Caning only lasted a few moments, but peeling vegetables—or worse, planting cassava in the school's gardens—could take a whole day. The dorm room was filling up with boys all trying to unpack as quickly as possible. Paul was getting very impatient.

"Enough." He booted Jacob's suitcase and bucket under the cot, then yelled, "Run!"

The three boys raced out of the dorm, bodychecking each other as they went.

They barged through the common room at the entrance of the dorm, jostling and nudging each other. Once outside, they raced across the grass, kicking an imaginary football between them. Their laughter mixed with the noise from one hundred and fifty students as they all tumbled into the chapel. Each made the sign of the cross at the end of the pew before shuffling along the row and plopping down on the hard bench. Hands covered mouths as they tried to muffle their giggles.

Paul nudged Jacob. "Over there. That's him."

There was no mistaking Norman. He sat by himself, shoulders slumped, eyes riveted on his feet.

"How did we get stuck with him?" Jacob grumbled to Paul. Then he looked around at all the boys, and instantly his spirits picked up. Maybe they were stuck with babysitting a twelve-year-old, but it didn't matter. The kid would find his own friends soon enough. This was going to be the best term ever.

Father Ricardo, the school's priest, said a prayer. Then Assistant Headmaster Otim welcomed them all back to the school and introduced Headmaster Heycoop.

The headmaster was a formidable man with a bus-sized torso and a pushed-in hippo head screwed onto a brick of a body. There were rumors that the headmaster had once been a heavyweight boxer before he'd heard the voice of God calling him to the priesthood, and after that to the seminary. He was almost deaf, so Jacob thought that God must have had to really yell.

"I have great news!" Headmaster bellowed. He compensated for not being able to hear by talking a lot, and talking loudly. "I am happy to announce that the building of our new library will commence immediately, with a completion date set for the new year. And the budget will allow us to buy a hundred new books." Headmaster Heycoop paused, allowing the *ohhh*s and *ahhh*s to subside.

Headmaster wasn't finished. "George Jones Seminary for Boys

exists to produce scholars who will take our great country of Uganda into the future. We must therefore avail ourselves of the world's knowledge, both past and present. Knowledge is infinite and waits patiently to be both discovered and rediscovered. And yet our lives are finite." Headmaster Heycoop's voice began to wobble, as though he might burst into song. *Please, no*, thought Jacob.

"From our country's long past, which touches Creation itself, to our greater future"—the headmaster stretched out his arms to embrace the air—"we who are in this House of God have mere moments to determine the truth before we are called back into the welcoming arms of our Creator. Now, let us pray."

They prayed. They sang. Headmaster Heycoop was the loudest. He was tone-deaf and threw everyone off. Paul started to giggle, then Tony, then Jacob, and finally the whole row of boys was shaking with laughter. Headmaster's arms went up and down with the music. The laughter was a fire spreading up and down the rows. Teachers stood up and shot angry glances, but how could one punish an entire school? Some of the boys managed to swallow their giggles, but not all.

With the last prayer, led by Father Ricardo, the laughter subsided and the congregation of boys murmured "Amen." Finally they all sang the closing hymn.

As soon as they could, the boys all leapt out of their seats. Paul and Tony were caught in a wave of students that bunched up at the door, pushing and shoving, calling out to each other, laughing, then spilling out of the chapel.

Jacob pressed himself against the wall and waited. He might as well say something to the new boy and get it over with. As Norman moved along with the crowd, Jacob elbowed his way toward him.

"Hi, I'm Jacob."

Norman looked up, eyes wide, lips slightly parted, as if he were about to yell or make a run for it. *I know he's twelve,* Jacob thought, *but he looks ten … nine, even.* And just as Jacob had suspected, there were tears circling in the boy's eyes.

"You like mathematics?" Jacob was almost yelling now as the crowd of boys surged around them.

The boy nodded.

"Know your times tables?"

Again the boy nodded, and for a fleeting second there might have been the hint of a smile. No, it was more of a grimace, as though someone was stepping on his foot. Wait, someone *was* stepping on his foot.

"Hi." Tony leapt up and hollered over Paul's shoulder.

The two had managed to worm their way back through the crowd. "I'm Tony. This is Paul."

"We hear that you are good in math." Paul nudged Jacob. "Give him a question."

It seemed a little mean. Jacob shrugged, but he figured he might as well put this Norman kid in his place as soon as possible.

"What is 981 times 97?" Paul and Tony snickered.

Startled, Norman looked up at Jacob. His eyes narrowed. Jacob sucked in air. *He's seeing the numbers,* he thought. Speaking slowly, his lips barely moving, Norman enunciated one number at a time: "Nine, five, one, five, seven."

"*Atoo tin!*" Jacob muttered under his breath. Normally he did not swear.

▪▪▪

The three boys sat on Jacob's bed, with a jar of peanut butter to share. The school's evening meal of *potio* might have filled their stomachs, but it hadn't left them any less hungry. It was the only thing about school that Jacob really didn't like—the food.

"Look at him," said Paul.

The three glanced over at Norman. Despite only one meager, bald, dim light bulb dangling from an overhead beam in the middle of the dormitory, Norman sat on his bed with his knees up and his head buried in a book. Jacob sighed. They should do something with him, talk to him maybe, include him. They had promised.

"We'll take him to class with us tomorrow," suggested Tony.

Jacob and Paul nodded vigorously. The idea eased their guilt. They would make friends with the new kid tomorrow.

Jacob carried on with his story.

"So the two bulls charged at each other, and the head boy yelled so loud he fell out of the tree!" Jacob could hardly finish his tale about school break before convulsing with laughter.

Paul had the most exciting story of all. He told them about his father, about how he had stood in front of many important people in America and given a speech. He was obviously very proud of his father, Jacob thought, although he was trying not to show it. Paul didn't want to look like a show-off. None of them did.

"Tell us about America!" Jacob prompted him.

"Well, in New York City there is a team called the Yankees. They play a game with a hard white ball and bat, like cricket but not at all like cricket. They play at night but it looks like day."

Jacob and Tony nodded their heads, although neither understood. Night was night. How could night be day?

"And there are moving staircases, and they eat dogs in buns. And Jacob, your father has many bulls on his farm, but I drank Red Bull in a can." Paul howled with laughter at that.

Tony and Jacob sat confounded. Liquid animal juice? Blood? Did Americans drink bulls' blood out of a can?

"And the telephones are attached to the wall with a wire."

Wires on a telephone? How could it fit into a pocket?

"Are American streets filled with wires?" Jacob asked.

"No. There are telephones that are attached to the walls, and they have cellphones too." Paul said all this with great authority, but still none of it made sense. Lots of people in Africa had cellphones, lots and lots. But why would Americans need *two* kinds of phones?

Jacob looked at Tony. "So, what did you do on your holiday?" he asked.

"I read the entire book of Matthew in Italian. Father Ricardo suggested that I study Italian. After all, the Vatican is in Rome." Tony stopped, looked down at his hands, and started to mumble. "I mean, if I ever went to Rome, it would be ...." Paul and Jacob plastered perplexed looks on their faces, which made Tony stumble even more.

Jacob tried not to laugh. Everyone knew that Tony wanted to become a priest—Tony, always last to leave chapel and first to raise his hand in religious studies class. Did he really think his friends didn't know?

The peanut butter jar was licked clean and Paul's crackers—meant to last the whole term, or at least the week—were almost gone before the boys said their prayers and crawled into bed. Some of the boys in the dorm wore nightclothes, although most, like Tony, wore their school shirts and shorts to bed.

The prefect flicked off the overhead light and the humming generator outside the barred window was instantly silenced. The lock on the door clicked. The boys were locked in to prevent them from running off in the night to the girls' convent school a few kilometers down the road. That's what they were told, although not once had Jacob known anyone to do such a thing. There was a deadbolt on the inside door too but no one bothered with it.

Jacob lay in the dark, hands behind his head, and thought that he couldn't have been happier. Once, old Bella had said that cooking made her happy because it allowed her to share her happiness. It was true, he thought. A person could be content alone, maybe even at peace, but happiness was real only if it was shared.

Someone farted. The dorm erupted in laughter.

"Put it back! Put it back!" yelled someone down the row of beds. Then another voice in the dark, "Farts can't be caught."

The whole dorm roared with laughter all over again. The prefects didn't barge in and turn on the light. Even the prefects this year were great. It took a while for everyone to settle down again.

"Paul," Jacob whispered across the space between their two beds, "what was it like to fly in the air across the ocean?"

"I was scared, very scared. But I did not want to embarrass myself so I did what my father did."

"What is the food like in America?" Tony leaned out of his own bed.

"Very bad. It tastes like dust and comes in packages." Jacob was not surprised. People from America, Canada, and even England and Australia sent food over to Africa that tasted terrible. He thought that maybe they sent only the food they refused to eat, but maybe their food really was terrible. Maybe they did not know how to cook.

"But many American people are very fat," said Jacob. He had seen many pictures and he wasn't being mean. He admired fat. "If their food is so bad, why are they so big?"

"They eat a great deal of the bad food and there is much food available. It is hard to explain their markets that they call *super* ..." Paul's voice faded for a moment. "I think that even when they are full, they eat," was all he could think to say.

"Do they *all* eat twice a day?" Tony's voice rose up in amazement.

"More than that. Maybe three, four, five times a day. They call it *snack*," he said quietly.

"What is *snack*?" asked Tony. They were taught English but none had come across such a word.

"I do not know," said Paul.

None spoke for a moment.

"Do they all smell sweet?" Despite his amazement Tony could not stop his questions.

"Even the black people in America smell white!" laughed Paul.

Jacob, who was listening intently, flopped back on his mattress, stared at the ceiling, and tried to picture the sweet-smelling fat people, telephones attached to walls, and wires hanging out of pockets. The full moon shining through the barred window cast stripy lines on his bed. Smiling, Jacob drifted off to sleep.

It was two o'clock in the morning when the entire dorm awoke to the sound of gunshots.

7
ABDUCTION

Every boy bolted upright at the same time. The terror was immediate.

Bang, bang, bang. Somebody was hammering at their door, over and over, smashing it as hard as they could.

"LRA," one boy after another hissed. "LRA." It did not have to be said. No one had to be told. They all knew it. They all felt it. "LRA, LRA, LRA."

Rebels? How? Jacob, sitting, stiff, peered into the dark. Father had arranged for extra guards. They were safe. *Safe.* How could this be?

The dormitory was partly lit by the full moon that shone through the windows.

Bang, bang, bang.

Jacob looked to the door. It seemed to pulse, in and out, as if it were breathing.

"The lock won't hold," yelled Paul.

Bang, bang, bang—the sound reverberated around the room. Some boys crawled under their beds and curled up like snails. Others stayed put and drew their knees to their chests.

"Bolt it!" yelled Paul. Out of the corner of his eye Jacob caught a glimpse of Paul at a window.

Whatever ingenuity Jacob had came to him now. Using the bed as a springboard he vaulted toward the door. He couldn't see; he stumbled. His hands pawed the wooden door as he slid to the floor.

Face down, Jacob could hear footsteps on the other side of the door. *Thud, thud, thud*—the steps echoed as if an army of hundreds was about to trample them underfoot. Shouting, lots of shouting. He couldn't make out the words over the sound of his heart pounding in time with the hammering of footsteps.

"Jacob, the bolt!"

Who was that? Paul? Again a club, or maybe a rifle butt, hit the door. He reached up and slid the bolt into place. *Thunk.* The sound was reassuring and for a moment there was protection, safety, hope.

Jacob, still on the floor, looked up. He could see Norman's small body sway as if caught in a whirling wind. Then *bang, bang, bang.* The door was being rammed by something larger than a rifle butt now.

Paul, Tony, and a bunch of boys were pulling at the bars on the window. Tony placed his feet on the wall. With his hands reaching for the bars between his legs, he strained. He made desperate, guttural, animal sounds. Moonlight bounced off the muscles popping on his neck, but still the bars wouldn't budge.

The thumping stopped. Another silence, but this one lasted longer. A communal holding of breath. Perhaps the soldiers had turned their attention to one of the other dorm rooms? Perhaps? Perhaps?

The moment passed. An axe splintered the door.

"Get dressed." Paul's voice was somewhere between a scream and a guttural hiss. "Dress. Get dressed!"

Snapped out of a trance, Jacob and Tony scrambled toward their lockers and pulled on shirts and sweaters. Shoes, they needed shoes most of all. A few boys did likewise, but many, like Norman, were paralyzed with fear.

"Dress!" Jacob yelled. Nothing seemed to shake Norman out of his stupor. Jacob opened the boy's locker, picked up a pair of shorts and a sweater, and tossed them at him. "Shoes, put on your shoes!"

First the axe created a sliver, then a slit, then an opening. What little moonlight there was filtered through the window and shone on the hole in the door. The hole widened and through it came a dirty hand. The disembodied hand flopped about, found the bolt, and yanked it back. The door opened with a crash. Windup flashlights scanned the room like searchlights, settling on one terrified face then another and another and another. The overhead light was flicked on. Outside the generator sprang to life.

A moment passed before Jacob's eyes adjusted to the overhead light. Standing on the threshold was the LRA— the Lord's Resistance Army.

An unnatural quiet settled as the soldiers swaggered down past the beds. Some smiled, others laughed; most were grim-faced.

"ATTENTION!"

The boys tried to stand tall, all in different states of dress.

"My name is Commander Opiro. Do I have your attention?" Commander Opiro—perhaps twenty-five years old, but who could tell?—wearing dreadlocks and dressed in dirty camouflage clothes, paused. "If anyone cries or screams for any reason he will be punished by death. Do you understand?" Opiro, who had begun by yelling, suddenly lowered his voice and spoke softly, as if he were telling children a bedtime story. "And when you are dead, you will better understand."

He stopped in front of Jacob. Spit crackled in his mouth as he peered into Jacob's eyes. Jacob tried to look away but Opiro stuck the barrel of his gun under Jacob's chin. Eyes wide, heart pounding, Jacob looked into black, smiling eyes.

"You will be soldiers now. You will fight for your country and kill for God."

Casually, almost indifferently, Opiro slung his gun over one shoulder then sauntered down the line of students, looking them up and down as if browsing in a market. The rest of them, the other soldiers, leaned against the walls. They looked bored. The more energetic soldiers kicked open the boys' lockers and rifled the contents.

Panic has a way of keeping reality at bay, but now Jacob felt his lungs being squeezed and air being cut off. The room began to reel. He wanted to steady himself but was afraid to reach out, terrified that any movement might draw the soldiers' attention.

A cellphone rang. Commander Opiro answered it. He said "Yes" three times then snapped the phone shut. Down the line of beds a cheer went up as a soldier unearthed a stash of peanut butter from a student's locker. He twisted off the lid and plunged his hand into the jar, then slopped the brown goop into his mouth.

"This yours? Did your mother make this?"

Jacob did not turn his head but he was pretty sure the soldier was talking to Arthur—a good boy who wanted to drive a car one day. Last term all he'd talked about was cars. The soldier stuck out a pink tongue and licked the side of the peanut butter jar. Jacob turned his head just a little. Laughter spilled out of the mouths of the soldiers like poisonous drool as urine ran down Arthur's leg.

"Look!" The soldier pointed to the puddle between Arthur's feet. More laughter.

With the soldiers' attention diverted, Jacob balanced himself against a bedframe. He dared not look at Paul or Tony, and he was afraid to look at Norman, afraid that the boy would do something stupid.

Think, think. There were ten or more soldiers in the room, more in the common room. Had they broken into any other dorms? Had they killed the guards? How many rebel soldiers were outside? Most of the rebels' guns were small and lightweight, but others looked as if they could kill an elephant, two elephants! Jacob had never seen such guns, not up close. Some soldiers cradled their guns like treasured babies, others carried them as if they were extensions of their arms and hands. Bullets hung around their necks like rows of beads, and their clothes were rags. Many wore cast-off army fatigues, others wore T-shirts or tank tops with names of athletic shoes sprawled across their chests. Most had green or black gumboots, while others wore military boots with broken laces and flapping tongues. As they walked down the line, past the boys and beds, they left a trail of stink.

Something was odd about these rebel soldiers. Jacob looked closer. Several of them wore filthy and torn tank tops. They held their guns high. His mouth dropped open. There was no hair under their arms. Kids! Children with guns, some younger than himself. Carefully, without moving his head too quickly, Jacob glanced from one soldier to the next and the next. There were only two adult soldiers in the room: the one who called himself Commander Opiro, and his second-in-command, who also looked to be in his early twenties. Jacob knew the LRA used boy soldiers, but only a few, not this, not everyone.

"What are you looking at?" A soldier pivoted in front of Jacob. He couldn't have been more than thirteen years old. Long, grotesque gashes lined his face. They were old wounds, healed mostly, leaving raised, dark ridges up and down his cheeks. It was as if someone had haphazardly dragged a trowel across his face. His eyes were bloodshot and blank, as though he wasn't really looking at anything, like he was blind. No, not blind, it was as if he couldn't *see.*

"I said, what are you looking at?"

"Nothing," Jacob whispered. Should he call him "sir"? There was another soldier standing behind this disfigured thirteen-year-old. Was he thirteen?

The soldier behind the scarred boy soldier was tall, taller than Paul. His hair was short and his face was sculpted, with high cheekbones and sloping almond-shaped eyes. There was something familiar about him. His eyes were glued to Jacob's face. Jacob tried to take a good look. The tall boy was staring. It was as if he was saying to Jacob: *Shut up, shut up, shut up.*

"Nothing? You see nothing?" the thirteen-year-old yelled. The tall soldier, the one with the high cheekbones, receded, then disappeared from view.

That's it! The boy from the church. It was him! Jacob was sure of it. What was his name? It was hard to think, let alone remember. Yes, it was Oteka. Jacob wanted to reach out, to touch him, to say something, anything. But this Oteka was a rebel, a soldier, the enemy. Then why was he talking to him with his eyes?

"Nothing, sir." Jacob immediately cast his own eyes down. He was in that position, eyes staring at his shoes, when the rifle butt smashed into the side of his head. And then came a flash of white light.

8
PUNISHMENT BY DEATH

"Quiet. Jacob, do not make any sound." The voice was distant.

Jacob tried to open his eyes. He moaned. "Quiet, Jacob, be quiet."

There was a hand over his mouth. Had he embarrassed himself? Had he had a nightmare? Had he woken up the other boys in the dorm? His head throbbed. He had to sit up. He should ask the school nurse for an Aspirin tablet.

"Jacob."

That was Tony's voice. Why was Tony hissing in his ear?

"Jacob, you must wake up." Another voice. Was it Paul's? Jacob tried to form Paul's name but his mouth felt as if he had been chewing on wood.

"Listen to me, Jacob, you must open your eyes. YOU MUST. Please, Jacob."

Who said that? Who was speaking now? Sunlight. He opened his eyes then snapped them shut. There was clapping. Who was clapping? It was faint at first but it grew louder and louder. Oh, his head! He drew his hands up to his ears. Stop. Stop. His eyelashes were stuck together. He pulled his eyelids apart, but what he saw made no sense. It wasn't quite daybreak but there was light. Above him, tree branches intertwined. The trees were holding hands and dancing. His tongue was too big for his mouth. Water, he wanted water.

"Walk, Jacob. You must walk."

Tony and Paul crouched on either side of him. Up, up. He was on his feet but couldn't feel the ground. No, no, he wanted to lie down. His head lolled from side to side and his knees buckled so he fell back into the dirt. As the dancing trees shivered something black came over him. A cloud? A wave? His memory was broken into bits. He did not see the boot coming. It missed his ribs and hit his belly. Jacob clutched his middle and moaned.

"He walks on his own or he's dead."

With balled-up fists, Jacob rubbed his eyes and watched the green heels of oversized gumboots shuffle away down a path. He slammed his eyes shut.

It wasn't a nightmare, but it wasn't real, either. "Jacob, are you all right?"

Was that Ethel? No, Ethel was at home. Again Jacob tried to open his eyes but the sunlight was as sharp as daggers. He saw Paul first. He was dirty, his face smeared with dirt.

"Ohh, ohh."

Who had said that? He had said that! He was going to vomit. As soon as Jacob opened his mouth, Tony's hand covered it.

"Don't make any sound. They will kill you if you make any noise. Promise?" Tony was hissing in his ear. *Promise?* Promise what? Tony's hand was suffocating him.

"Away, away." Jacob tried to bat Tony's hand back. Why wouldn't he take his hand away? Jacob swallowed hard. Breathe, breathe.

"Promise?" Tony hissed in his ear. Jacob nodded.

With each movement a piercing pain shot up his neck—there was fire in his head. Slowly, he turned and looked to one side. A sort of gunnysack and a pole lay on the ground—the kind of thing a sick person might be carried in.

"Where are we? What …?" Jacob gasped for air. Water, he needed water.

"We don't know. In the bush. We just followed." Paul's words were short, as if he was afraid. But of what?

"My head ..." Jacob moaned.

"You got hit and we couldn't wake you up. They were going to kill you. That soldier, the one with the scarred face, he's mean. They call him Lizard." Paul was babbling into his ear. "One of the old guys, they call him Commander, asked who you were. I told him your name. He said that you looked fit so they made us carry you. We carried you all night," hissed Paul.

"Lizard—he's out for you, Jacob. The commander, the one who said that you should live, he has gone somewhere else. You have to walk on your own, you have to." Now Tony was talking.

Jacob wanted to reach out, to tell him that they were all happy that he would become a priest. But why were they talking about a lizard? A lizard was a harmless gecko, a useless reptile, a pest that scampered up walls. Jacob couldn't make sense of it.

"Please, Jacob, don't let them kill you," Tony whispered in Jacob's other ear. Jacob looked up. Elephant tears dribbled down Tony's face. They ran into the dirt there and created wiggle lines down his cheeks.

There was something shiny drawn on Tony's forehead. Jacob looked over to Paul. What was that—it was on his forehead too. Jacob's arm felt like lead but he lifted it and tried to touch the spot on Paul's head.

"They traced crosses on us with shea nut oil. They said that we are now 'soldiers of the movement.' See?" Paul picked up Jacob's hand and traced the cross drawn on Jacob's own forehead. Tony was mumbling something, a prayer maybe: "Sweet Jesus, help us in our hour of need." Jacob snapped back his hand. His fingers were greasy. Tears careened down Tony's face.

"Stop crying, Tony, stop, stop," whispered Jacob. If the other boys in school saw him cry he'd get bullied for sure. Jacob looked over to Paul, and then saw Norman sitting on his haunches, wide-eyed and silent. He remembered little Norman who was good in math. They had promised to take care of him. Lights out in the dorm. Sleep. Pounding on the door.

Jacob's eyes darted from Tony to Paul to Norman and back to Tony. "Where are our teachers?"

"There are no teachers here." Tony was growing frustrated. He repeated what Paul had just said … *hit on the head … dragged through the bush … must walk.* Slowly, painfully slowly, Tony's words registered.

Still confused, Jacob uttered, "Why did they let this happen?"

"Mr. Ojok—we walked past him. He was lying on the ground. Maybe he was dead. We did not see any other teachers." Paul's voice was low, raspy, as if he had spent hours cheering at a football match.

"What about the guards?" There were extra guards hired. Father had arranged it.

"They ran away."

Ethel. Ethel had said that paying the guard was a waste of money. What did she say? *Run away … Kony's Lord's Resistance Army coming down the road.* Why couldn't he think straight?

"Get up. It's time to march." A command came down the line.

As Jacob snapped his head back another searing pain shot up his neck.

"I said, get up and march!" The voice was loud and squeaky at the same time—the voice of a boy.

What had Tony called this young rebel? Lizard? With help from Tony and Paul, Jacob staggered up onto two shaky legs.

"You walk on your own or you die." Lizard stopped shouting and hissed like a snake, "If it were up to me, you would be dead now, but they say that you have value. We shall see." Lizard stood back, adjusted his gun, and spoke to all the boys within earshot. "Do not help him. He is not your friend. No one is your friend." He looked at the four boys with disgust. "Soon you will learn."

A soldier in the distance called out an order. Lizard waved to him, then walked away.

The four staggered on into the bush, walking as if linked by an invisible chain. Paul led their small band, Jacob came next, then Norman, then Tony, at the end. Ahead and behind were the rest of the students of the George Jones Seminary for Boys, all shuffling along, all exhausted and in a state of shock.

As Jacob walked, an image came back to him, a flash of a face. Very tall. Sloped eyes. Wide mouth. The boy from the church. Oteka. Had he dreamed seeing him? What could he be doing here?

Step, step, step. Jacob counted out the number of students. There were thirty-eight in the dorm. His head pounded and his stomach quaked. Step, step, step. Just keep walking. All thirty-eight boys had families that would come after them. His own father would come, he was sure of it. Even now his father was coming. And there were the government soldiers. They would be coming, too. It wouldn't be long. They just had to stay alive, and do what they were told. It would be all right. Just put one foot in front of the other. Rescue was on the way.

9
TONY

No water. Jacob's thirst was overpowering now. His tongue grew swollen and his throat tightened. It was hard to swallow. Worse, his eyes were playing tricks on him—the ground rose up and down and the path kept changing shape. He stumbled constantly and fell many times.

"Do you want to rest?" a soldier asked, his lips pulled back over shining teeth. Rest, yes, he wanted to rest. Yes please, more than anything.

"We want to walk." Tony gave Jacob a gentle push from behind.

"Rest?" Jacob mumbled.

"To *rest* means to *die*," Tony hissed back. The boys had learned much while Jacob slept.

They walked in silence. No one spoke above a hiss and orders seemed to be understood rather than spoken. The rebel soldiers fingered their guns as if itching to kill. Why hold back? Why not kill them all? What was this for? Jacob tried to calculate the kilometers covered—maybe twenty, maybe more? But then there were the kilometers walked when he was unconscious. It was confusing.

Why had he not listened to his father and his father's friends? The rebels, the Lord's Resistance Army, called themselves Christians. Kony was their leader. That much Jacob knew for sure. Kony said that he wanted to free the Acholi people and create an Acholi homeland. Was that true? Yes, he was almost sure. They recruited their fighters from schools, transports, and villages, then made the children fight government soldiers. But what if they just said no? What if they refused to fight?

That day they trudged through banana plantations and fought their way through bush and thickets that left tiny slivers in their flesh. The sun beat down and sweat bubbled up on the skin and stuck like mud. Fields suddenly turned into swampland. Mosquitoes feasted on them. They passed through blade-sharp elephant grass and overgrown pathways. They crossed broken railway tracks. Hisses came down the line: "Walk in the tracks of the person ahead. The entire area is covered in land mines. Don't leave the column." Was it a trick to keep them from running off, or was it true?

Jackfruit trees, scrub, criss-crossed paths, a burnt-out village with crumbling huts and caved-in roofs. Jacob's eyes were in a constant squint. Something winked in the sunlight—a steel water tower on its side. He tried to take note of his surroundings, find markers so that he could make his way back. It was no use. He was disoriented. It seemed as though they were walking in circles, but that made no sense if the LRA was trying to put as much distance as possible between the students and their rescuers.

Blinking, Jacob looked up at the sky. Blue and still, it was a day to play football, listen to stories under an *owii* tree, or sit in a classroom beside tall, open windows and feel a gentle breeze.

Father, where are you? Where are the government soldiers? Where are the gunship helicopters and the great army with its modern weapons? Why haven't you come after us yet? We can't be that hard to find!

"There's a village ahead." Information was passed down the line in hisses and whispers. Maybe there they could rest? *Please, please, God, we need rest.*

They arrived at a village, but not a village. There were round mud huts with straw roofs. Women and very small children milled about, but where were the elders? It didn't *feel* like a village. No clotheslines, no *kolos* in front of the huts, no pots on the boil, no piles of cassava. And there was a smell to the place, an awful sickly-sweet stench that scorched the inside of the nose and throat.

More women with babies on their hips emerged from huts and stared at the new arrivals. Little children tottered around with big bellies, and stringy legs and arms. Their oversized heads, crowned with rust-tinged bristles, wobbled on spindly stems. The smallest babies lay naked and unattended on dirty goatskins. And their ears were black. Not black—Jacob looked harder—their ears were infested with ear mites.

He looked more closely at the women. They had babies on their hips but they weren't really women, they were girls, almost children themselves, dressed in filthy *busutis* or worn-out school uniforms. Most were barefoot, but some wore rubber *sapatu* on dirty feet. The young mothers watched wide-eyed as the new recruits were paraded past them.

Jacob heard the sound of an engine, a truck, maybe. "Tony," he hissed.

Tony waved him away with the back of his hand, then rubbed his face. He was crying.

Norman crept up behind Jacob, stepping on his heels. They had promised to take care of Norman, but how could they when they couldn't even take care of themselves? Jacob turned his back to Norman and riveted his eyes to the ground. He willed Norman to go away. The boy must have sensed something because he backed away. When next Jacob caught a glimpse of him, Norman looked smaller than his twelve years, much smaller, and very alone. Jacob felt bad but there was nothing he could do, why couldn't the kid see that?

An ancient Jeep rumbled down a rutty path, stopping in the middle of the village. Commander Opiro jumped out, picked up his gun, and draped it casually across his back. He rocked on his heels and surveyed his catch. He looked well-fed and wore mismatched army pants and shirt. A black belt divided his two halves, a filthy red scarf encircled his neck, and black aviator glasses hid his eyes. He was as dirty as a rat.

"Line up straight, like soldiers." After the long silence of their walk, the commander's voice seemed extra loud. The students of George Jones Seminary for Boys formed a wiggly line. Norman stood on one side of Jacob, Paul on the other, and Tony beside Paul.

"You are rebels now. You fight for freedom. You fight for the Lord's Resistance Army and for God. Kony is our leader and we do what he says." Commander Opiro looked at the boys in front of him then spat on the ground. "I shall tell you the rules and you will listen. You are fighters, and fighters must know the rules." He paused again, then took a deep breath. "You must not fight with food in your mouth. Stones have great power. You must not urinate on stones, and do not shout across a river. Do not use stones to make fire or the stones may explode. Do not fear the bullets from a government gun. Their guns are weak and the bullets will bounce off you like hard rain. A Jesus cross drawn on your body with oil will also prevent bullets from hurting you. You must not touch alcohol or any drugs. We are all Christians and we must obey the Ten Commandments. Now, I ask you, do you like women?" He jammed his thumbs into his belt as dusty dreadlocks danced on his shoulders.

Panic spread down the line. What was the right answer? Yes meant no. No meant what? Death?

"You see these women?" The commander pointed to the girls standing off in the distance. "These women are wives of soldiers.

If any of you are caught *talking* to any woman, the woman will be killed and you will be beaten." He paused. "Now, I will tell you a most important rule. You will listen. You will see what it means to break a law." He snapped his fingers in the air.

A girl wearing a scarf emerged from a hut. She was tall and strong looking, maybe fourteen years old. Dark skin, knobby legs, slender, a high forehead, thin nose—black eyes with hints of gold, tiger-eyes.

He snapped his fingers again and she moved sideways until she stood beside Commander Opiro.

"I will show you what happens to anyone who tries to escape. I show you what we will do to you *if you are lucky*." He yanked the scarf from her head.

Everyone, Jacob included, drew in a deep breath.

Her ears had been cut off.

"This girl might have been given to a commander; maybe she'd have become a wife to Kony himself. But look at her now. She is worthless. She is nothing. No man would touch her. If you try and run away I will do the same to you, or worse." He laughed.

A boy at the front of the line folded in half, then dropped to his knees. Had he fainted? Jacob kept his head facing forward but moved his eyes. It was Adam. He and Paul ran long-distance races together. Adam always won the school races. He was the school's football star, too. It was rumored that he would play for the national team in Kampala next year. There were even whispers about him trying out for the Olympic team. He was an only child, the pride of his parents. Adam was known for his stamina.

"What is wrong with him?" Jacob hissed.

"A soldier … hit … broken ribs, maybe," Paul whispered, as loudly as he dared. No one but Jacob heard. All attention was on Adam.

"Get up, get up," Jacob hissed under his breath. *Please, God. Please, God.*

A student reached out to help Adam.

"Do not touch him," bellowed Opiro. "You touch him and you suffer his fate."

Fate? What fate? He was wounded. He needed help. Soldiers got treatment, didn't they? Help him! The voices inside Jacob's head were screaming: *Why? Why?*

Some girls picked up their babies and bounced them up and down on their hips, while others sat on the ground with their legs curled under them, as if waiting for a spectacle to begin. There were chairs, but none of the girls made use of them. Jacob turned back to look at the girl without ears but she had vanished.

A young soldier shoved the kneeling Adam onto the ground. Sprawled out, clutching his side, he looked so vulnerable. A sound was coming out of his mouth—not a cry, more like a gurgle. And then he fell forward. Adam had passed out.

Stop this! Stop this! The words banged around in Jacob's head.

"You, you, you …" shouted the commander as he arbitrarily selected five boys from the line of students. "I need one more." He looked over at Jacob, paused, and, with a caustic grin, pointed to Tony instead. With his hand still extended, the commander motioned toward a stack of short logs on the ground. The boys stared, blank-eyed, at the logs, then turned and looked at each other. What were they supposed to do with logs?

"Kill or be killed!" roared the commander. And then they all understood. They were to beat Adam to death.

"I am a Catholic. It is God's commandment that I not kill. *Thou shalt not kill,*" said Tony. He was bold and confident.

No, no, no! Jacob drew in a breath and balled up his fists. The students riveted their eyes on the commander as he raised his gun and pointed it at Tony's head.

Tony did not flinch. His face looked trouble-free.

My friend, my friend. The words raced around Jacob's head.

Commander Opiro turned. His smile was like a snake slowly crawling across his face. The obscene grin revealed brown nubs of teeth buried in black gums. No one moved. Jacob's skin went cold while his body burned. Shock, they were all in shock.

Commander Opiro laughed and nodded to two rebel soldiers in his command. The soldiers stepped forward and grabbed Tony by the arms. What were they going to do?

Tony's feet left long skid marks in the dust as they dragged him over to a big tree trunk. One soldier stood behind Tony and held him by the waist. The other grabbed Tony's left arm and stretched it out over the tree. A third soldier stepped forward and raised a *panga* above his head. Tony's arm would come off!

"No, no!" His head swivelled to one soldier, then the next. "No, please, no!" Tony cried. Paul was about to lurch forward when Jacob grabbed his tattered shirttail. Paul moaned.

"Wait," Jacob whispered. They had to think, not act. "Would you prefer a long-sleeved or short-sleeved shirt?" The soldier holding the *panga* laughed.

What did he mean? The boys looked from one to the other.

"If you would like a long-sleeved shirt we will take off your hand, but if you would like a short-sleeved shirt we will take off your arm," said the soldier. For effect he smashed the *panga* into the tree trunk, sending splinters of wood flying off in all directions.

"NO!" Tony was terrified, and the whites of his eyes were as big as his whole face. "Our Father, who art in heaven ...." He cried and tried to squirm away but was held firm. "Hallowed be thy ...."

"It doesn't matter, you know." The commander bent down and spoke softly into Tony's ear, but all could hear well enough. "Your friend will die no matter what you do. He is injured. He is of no use. You will lose an arm and he will die, or you will not lose an arm and he will die. Here, we are fair. Here, we allow you to decide your own fate." The commander stood up straight and looked at all the boys. "What will it be?"

"Do not take my arm." Tony's whisper had turned into a whimper.

"Let him go," laughed the commander.

Stunned, traumatized, Tony fell to the ground, then scurried on all fours toward the five remaining boys, who stood quaking. Each held a log. Tony picked up one too.

Chanting started. Jacob looked over to the girls and their babies. Some danced, swirling their feet in the dust, arms extended and fluttering through the air. Others just sat and bobbed their heads. The girl with no ears was nowhere to be seen.

"You go first." The commander motioned toward Tony.

Not Tony. Tony who wants to be a priest. Dear God, help us in our hour of need .... Tears ran down Jacob's cheeks. He closed his eyes.

"Why do you close your eyes? You look away again and you will be punished by death." Lizard, standing in front of Jacob, pointed his gun between Jacob's eyes. Lizard wore an oversized tank top with long armholes that stretched almost to his waist. Like his face, the boy's back was severely marked. Long, deep slashes had healed badly, creating rivers of scars.

Slowly, Lizard walked behind Jacob and lodged the nub of his gun barrel in the base of Jacob's neck. "You watch or you die."

Tony shuffled across the sand and stood over the wounded boy. Adam lay unconscious in the sand. He twitched. A boy holding a log vomited down his shirt.

"Throw water on him. Wake him up." The commander was pointing to Adam, who lay motionless on the ground.

"No!" Tony screamed. His eyes rolled back in his skull. He howled like a beast, lifted the log above his head, and sent it crashing down. Then Tony fell onto his knees and covered his face with his hands.

"You, you ..." The commander pointed at one boy, then another. The boys converged on Adam. The women sang. Madness set in.

Think of the long-horned Ankoles, the Jerseys and Friesians. Think of climbing up a tree and watching the cows race. Think of laughing. Think of home.

10
GOD

Adam was dead. Time whirled and swirled around Jacob. It ebbed and flowed, grew into a mountain, and crashed down on him like a giant, rough wave. As soldiers cheered and young mothers danced, Jacob stood motionless.

Commander Opiro held up his hand and waited for silence. It came in an instant.

"Straighten this line."

The boys scrambled to do as they were told. Commander Opiro stood front and center and rocked on his heels, hands clasped behind his back.

"This boy here." The commander kicked Adam's body. "Why did this boy have to be killed?" He paused as if waiting for an answer. When none was offered he carried on. "He was killed because he was wounded and weak. God only wants strong soldiers to march for Him. We are at war. We are fighting to defend your country. You have not joined us by your own free will, even though we fight for you, so we will force you to do your duty."

The commander paced back and forth, tapping his fingers on the handgun in his holster.

"Only soldiers eat. If you want to eat, you will join us. This is your choice. If you die of hunger, it is your choice. If you steal food, you will be killed. And do not think the government soldiers will save you. You will walk, walk, and walk. The government soldiers will not find you. Look around. See our women and our children? These are the pure children, born of LRA commanders. The day will come when these pure children will rule Acholiland."

Again he paused, caught his breath, then started again.

"We have existed a long time. Museveni calls himself the president of Uganda, but he has no power here. The Ugandan Army thinks they are strong. They have helicopters, trucks, tanks, and powerful missiles and guns but they have no victory. Why? BECAUSE GOD IS NOT ON THEIR SIDE. GOD IS ON OUR SIDE."

The commander held his fist in the air as the rebel soldiers lifted their guns and gave a great cheer. The commander paused and looked at each of the students with contempt. He took a breath, and continued.

"You have come from school so you think you are smart. You are not smart. You are stupid. You think that if you speak English here you will not be understood and can therefore plot your escape. But we are smarter. If you speak English, you will be killed. If you try and escape, you will be killed. If you do escape, the government soldiers will kill you. You belong to the Lord's Resistance Army. Let us pray."

Pray? One boy looked to another. Pray?

Rifle butts slammed into their backs. "On your knees." Jacob was too slow. Lizard slugged Jacob in the back of the head. He pitched forward and fell. The pain in his head returned with a vengeance.

"You must face the east to pray to God because that is where God lives," shouted Commander Opiro. "Hands together. Now lower your head until it touches the ground."

Why? This was a Muslim tradition. Jacob knew that. All the boys knew. Kony's Christianity was a stew. They prayed.

Ten minutes later they were ordered to stand and sing "Onward Christian Soldiers." Most of the boys knew the words by heart, and those that did not pretended. *"Onward, Christian soldiers, marching as to war, With the cross of Jesus going on before …"* Tony, breathless, eyes blank, sang loudest of all. Jacob caught a glimpse of Norman. The boy's mouth opened and closed but no words came out. Most of the boys clumped together; everyone knew each other. Norman was a new boy, he had no one. Lizard cocked his gun and pointed it at Jacob and Paul. They sang loudly.

When the last verse died on their lips, the commander spoke again. He looked up to the sky. His voice rose up to the heavens, his hands reached for the clouds. "You are in God's army now. If you fail to do your duty, if you fail God, you will burn in a fiery Hell forever. Now you will learn how to be soldiers."

The women stood and edged back toward the huts. Jacob's heart began to pound. The air seemed to still itself. How was it birds did not sing or animals chatter in this place? What did he mean, "Now you will learn how to be soldiers"?

"Listen to me." The voice was a hiss in Jacob's ear. Jacob twisted around to see the source of the voice. "Don't turn around. Just answer me. What is your name?"

Name? Jacob hesitated. "Jacob, my name is Jacob."

"Are you the boy from the church?"

"Yes. Oteka, is it you?" he whispered.

"Yes, it is me. Do as I say. You will be beaten but you will live if you do not cry out. It will only hurt in the beginning, but no matter what, do not make a sound. Tell your friends. Hear me; if you want to live, do not cry out."

A group of ragged soldiers emerged from the huts. Every one of them was carrying something—a stick, a piece of leather, a bit of bicycle chain, a length of vine coated in oil. None of the soldiers looked older than fifteen.

"Remove your shirts. All over the age of sixteen will receive thirty lashes. Those under sixteen will receive twenty-five lashes," shouted the commander.

"Paul," Jacob whispered. "Don't make a sound. Tell Tony." He turned his head. Where was Norman? Jacob cursed under his breath. The boy was not his problem. They were not friends. They had only just met! But where was he? And then another boy from school took a step forward. There was Norman, standing behind him. Jacob sidestepped toward him, keeping his eyes on the commander and Lizard. When he was close enough to be heard, Jacob hissed to Norman, "No matter what, do not cry out."

One student after another was forced down in the dirt. The only sounds after that were the swishes of the weapons as they slapped against skin.

Father, Father. Father, come.

11
NYUMA GEUKA

The sky lightened, even though the sun had not yet made an appearance. Jacob heard monkey chatter and bird twitter but there was no movement from the surrounding huts. There was no one about, no guards. Why bother with guards when not one of them could walk, let alone run away?

"Paul?" Jacob cried out, then lowered his voice. "Paul!" The smallest movement sent ripples of pain through his body.

"I am here," Paul mumbled.

"Tony?" Jacob whispered.

Paul lifted his head out of the dust and looked over at Tony. There were moans but no one spoke.

"Tony, is he alive?" Jacob spat out each word as if it were glass.

"Yes, I saw him move." Paul used all his strength to answer.

"Norman?" There was no answer. "Norman?" Jacob called out. Still no response. Then a mumble. He was alive too.

A jug of water sat in the dirt a few feet away. All he had to do was crawl toward it. Jacob started out, hand over hand, dragging his lower body as if he were paralyzed from the waist down. Each inch was a mile. Face, nose, eyes, mouth—all caked in dust. Hard to breathe.

His hands shook as he tipped the jug just a little. Water splashed over his face and dribbled into his mouth. The water stank of dung but no matter, he drank, vomited, then drank again. The jug left a trail in the sand as he dragged it back to the line of boys. And then he saw them, sniffing—a small pack of spotted hyenas, sloped backs, cat-like, powerful jaws. Jacob reared up and howled. They were not dead yet. The pack skulked away.

Norman lay face down, nails dug into the dirt, legs extended in the dust.

Jacob crawled toward him. "Norman, wake up." Jacob reached into the jug, cupped his hand, and splashed water on Norman's face. "Drink, drink. They will come for us." Jacob pushed his face against Norman's ear and sobbed, "Listen to me, the army, our fathers—they will come. Just drink." His arms quivered as he tipped the jug to Norman's lips. Norman didn't move; he just lay very still.

"Wake up!" Jacob's sob turned into a cry. He was just a kid, a stinking kid who was good at multiplication. "Norman, what is 66 times 15?" Jacob hissed into his ear.

Nothing. He said nothing.

"Tell me. TELL ME! 66 times 15? You can see them. I know that you can see them. Picture the numbers. SEE THEM! 66 times 15."

Norman coughed and squished his eyes shut. "990."

Jacob's head pounded. What was the answer? No matter. "Yes, yes, you're right. You got it right. Drink, now drink."

"I want to go home," Norman sobbed. It was the simple request of a child. And then it struck him.

"Norman, how old are you?"

"Ten."

Jacob swore under his breath. Ten years old, just a little kid. Mr. Ojok must have thought that if he lied about Norman's age the boys would be more likely to befriend him.

"Don't cry, don't cry. You must be quiet. Can you hear me? You must be quiet." Jacob looked down at Norman. It wasn't fair. How was he supposed to take care of a kid? What did he know about caring for anyone? He didn't have any brothers or sisters or even a pet. Jacob looked up to the morning sky. The air was still. He took a breath and the pain of drawing air into his lungs almost made him cry out. "Look, Norman, we will stick together, okay? Just do not make noise. Hear me?"

Slowly Norman nodded.

"Paul, drink." Again Jacob wiggled through the dust, cupped his hand under the spout of the jug, and dribbled the liquid into Paul's gaping mouth. Norman crawled alongside as if afraid to be more than a few inches away from Jacob. Paul gulped the foul liquid, then turned his face back into the ground.

"Listen. We have to stay together. We have to try to keep each other safe. We are brothers, we are family." Jacob reached for Paul's—then Norman's—hand. Jacob spoke as loudly as he dared. There was still no movement from the huts, but he could hear the peeps and squeaks of small children as they began to wake.

"Swear to God, swear to each other, swear that we are brothers." Jacob's voice was steady, although the pain in his back made it hard to breathe properly.

As best they could Paul and Norman bobbed their heads and mumbled, "I swear."

Jacob looked over at Tony. His mind told him that Tony was innocent, that in his place they might all have done what he did, but his heart said something else. He could not forget the sight of Tony raising the log over his head to kill Adam.

Soft clapping had begun. It was the girls' way of announcing that the day had started and it was time to walk. Jacob passed the water jug down the line. Each boy took a sip, then one by one they struggled to stand. With strength Jacob hadn't thought he had, he hauled Norman to his feet. Paul staggered up on his own. Again they formed a ragged line and began the parade out of the village and into the bush.

Nyuma geuka. Left right, left right. The words were hummed and lodged in the brain until it was difficult to hear what was actually said and what was thought.

The smell! Sickly sweet. What was it? The huts along the edge of the village had been burned to the ground, and only black rings in the dirt remained. Where were the people? *Oh God, no*. Jacob turned his eyes away.

Since Jacob had climbed into his bed at school, said his prayers, and thought about making the football team or winning the mathematics award, twenty-four hours had passed.

122 times 85 equals 10,370.
333 times 22 equals 7,326.
245 times 67 equals 16,415.

"Don't turn around. Take this and give it to your friends, only friends. Trust no one." As Jacob walked, Oteka had come up from behind and pushed herbs into his hand. Jacob said nothing. Without being told, he knew not to talk to Oteka, not directly.

Jacob lifted the herbs to his nose and sniffed. *Lwit oput* leaves. Ethel used them to brew a tea when he was sick. She said that it took away pain better than the white tablets the white doctor in town gave out. Jacob bit into the herb. Almost instantly his mouth went numb. He edged up to Norman, then Paul.

"No chewing," Jacob murmured as he slipped the herb into their hands. "Do not let them see you chew." He looked over at Tony, but Tony did not look up, or around. He just moved one foot in front of the other. He didn't seem to be in pain, at least not on the outside.

▪▪▪

The sun grew high in the sky. *Nyuma geuka.* Left right, left right.

It was late afternoon now. *Nyuma geuka.* Left right, left right.

They stopped to pray.

"On your knees, forehead on the ground. Face east."

Twice Jacob saw Oteka with the commanders. He was easy to spot, because he stood head and shoulders taller than the rest.

As night fell, the boys slumped against trees or crawled under bushes to sleep. Oteka squatted on the other side of Jacob's tree and whispered in the dark, "Do not turn around. Just listen. You must know what happens next. You must know how they attack. You must be prepared."

Jacob tensed. Norman was asleep, but he could see Paul shift in the shadows, awake and listening. Tony, where was Tony? He too was asleep, curled up like a cat. "How did you come to be here?" Jacob asked Oteka.

The question plagued Jacob.

"That does not matter now. You must listen. There are four brigades in Kony's army and a commander rules each one. Under his command are families, wives and children, and all the soldiers and slaves. Each commander is all-powerful and can kill anyone he chooses. Attacks on a village are always the same. Surround it, squeeze tight. Kill the very young and the very old. They have guns but use bullets only when necessary. Bullets are to fight government soldiers, not villagers. Often the old people are murdered where they sit, outside their huts." Oteka paused to listen for footsteps. He heard nothing and so carried on. "Sometimes every single person in the village is killed and their food is taken."

Jacob was sitting but he still felt light-headed, as if he might faint.

"But the villagers, I mean, do they fight back?" asked Jacob.

"A few try, but just seeing the automatic weapons makes them afraid. Most just accept their fate or are so dazed they cannot move. The bigger boys and girls are captured and made to carry off the food. The animals are stolen or killed. The rebels poison the wells so no one can live there anymore. Only the children who can become slaves, wives, or soldiers are taken. Some are traded to the Sudanese. You must know this, you must be prepared."

"We must run away," whispered Jacob. The girl with no ears had instilled fear in all of them, but what was that compared to what they now faced? "We could run to a village, warn them, and they would help us." Even as he said the words, Jacob felt the foolishness of the idea.

"Some villagers might help but most will not. Too much killing has been done by the rebels for villagers to trust."

Jacob tried to digest this information before asking, "Where are we? Why can the government soldiers not find us?" He was desperate. This didn't make sense.

"That is why we walk, all the time, never stopping, so the army cannot find us. But listen, this is most important. Do not stay too close to your friends. The rebels do not like you to have loyalties. Be careful when you talk to each other."

There was a snap of a branch. Jacob turned his head toward the sound as Oteka slipped back into the night.

"Oteka?" he hissed into the dark. Gone.

Paul moved closer to Jacob. "He is your friend?"

"I do not know. I think so."

"How do you know him?" asked Paul.

"I just know his name—Oteka."

"Why is he helping us?" Skepticism crept into Paul's voice.

“I helped him once, that is all. But what he says is true, I feel it,” whispered Jacob.

“I feel it too.”

Jacob leaned against the tree. Something Oteka had said came back to him. He’d hardly noticed it at the time. Oteka had said, “The rebels poison the wells so no one can live there anymore.”

“He does not think himself a rebel,” Jacob whispered.

“What did you say?” Paul’s voice was heavy with sleep.

“Nothing.”

Both boys fell silent, and after a while Paul slept. Jacob looked up to the stars. Listening to the old men in his father’s courtyard share their horror and sorrow about Kony, hearing Musa Henry Torac talk about his much-loved grandson, Jacob had felt nothing. Nothing for the children that the rebels stole, nothing for their misery or their deaths, nothing for the people they were forced to kill. He had only thought, *What has it to do with me? Why should I care?* Jacob covered his face with his hands. *I did not know. Forgive me, I did not care to know.*

12
TWO WEEKS LATER

There was a routine to their days. The clapping of hands announced that it was time to leave camp. Not once had they woken up in the morning and gone to sleep at night in the same place.

Nyuma geuka. Left right, left right.

As soldiers and students, girls and babies, slaves and goats trudged through the bush, Commander Opiro and his band of sergeants climbed into a truck with loppy tires and drove down rutted paths until they reached furrowed roads. From there the truck disappeared from view.

Scouts led the way through the bush. The scouts were small boys who were well-fed and ran fast. Some were paces ahead, some hours ahead. Everyone had a designated job. Jacob, Norman, and Paul were slaves, like most of the schoolboys. The slaves carried all manner of things: bed rolls, tents, cooking pots, spare guns without bullets, pails, chairs, old red plastic gasoline cans filled with gritty water, crates of live chickens. Wounded soldiers were carried in gunnysacks strung between poles. Most died of their wounds since there was no first aid; there was none to give. Anyone else who was hurt or wounded was left to die. Only soldiers were buried.

Jacob carried a jerry can filled with water—water they were not allowed to drink. Paul hoisted a battered suitcase on his head and held a pail of cow slop in his free hand. Norman was given the most difficult job—to carry a jug of oil. The jug was big, maybe thirty liters. It took two boys to hoist it up and place it on a coiled rope on Norman's head. It seemed to press down on him, making Norman appear even smaller than he really was. He looked like an ant scurrying under a load twice his size. Neither Jacob nor Paul had a way to lessen his burden.

The day was long, the walk endless. They needed to stop, to rest. "Jacob, water." Norman spoke like a runner after a long race, breathless and exhausted. Together Jacob and Paul lifted the jug of oil off Norman's head. Norman slumped forward. Jacob pulled leaves off the underbrush and held them up to Norman's mouth. The dew on the leaves had already evaporated, but Norman sucked the leaves anyway. Food, they needed food. They ate what they could scavenge along the way: insects, wild fruits, and lizards—difficult to catch and harder still to skin.

"Here." Jacob broke twigs off a tree. Norman stuck one in his mouth and bit down. They all sucked on wooden sticks to keep the hunger and thirst away.

Jacob saw something beyond the elephant grass. "Wait, I'll be back." He batted the grass aside and raced down a slippery path toward a muddy water hole. There he scooped up a handful of mud, and he ran back and used it to moisten Norman's cracked lips.

"Norman, it will be all right." Over and over Jacob whispered these words in Norman's ear, and sometimes Paul's ear, too. "Help is coming. We just have to wait."

The scouts kept returning with bad news. More and more villages they came upon had been abandoned and so there was no food to steal.

On days when a scout did return with the news that there was a village ahead, an assault team was formed and off they went into battle. Except that there was no real battle. They just killed the villagers and made off with their food, animals, and sometimes children. Some days they fought off government soldiers. Seldom were the schoolboys involved in these fights. Girls, small children, slaves, and those who had yet to prove themselves in battle were told to sit in the long elephant grass and wait. Since Commander Opiro was seldom around, Lizard and another rebel named Eddie gave the orders.

Tony and the other boys who had killed Adam had guns—and not little wooden training guns either: real guns. It was as if the commanders were trying to make them special, different from the students and different from the regular recruits who had to train for weeks before getting a real gun.

Tony slung his gun across his back and walked a few paces ahead of Jacob. The metal of the gun must have grown hot under the sun because Jacob could see blistered burn marks on Tony's neck and upper arms. The scouts had seen another village and Lizard ordered the assault team to move out. Tony was part of the team. He marched away with his head hanging down. It was hours before they came back, and when they did, Tony was more dirty and distant than ever.

"Tony?" Jacob tried to get his attention. Tony would not look him in the eye, would not even acknowledge his existence.

Oteka crouched in the elephant grass and motioned to Jacob. "Come, come," he hissed.

Jacob crawled toward him, head swivelling, eyes looking every which way.

"Do not trust him," Oteka said. "He is a rebel now." As always, Oteka would whisper news or warning then disappear.

During the day Tony walked behind Lizard but at night he always seemed to want to be near the boys from school. Maybe Oteka was right. Maybe Tony could not be trusted. Maybe Tony *was* spying on them, but … maybe not.

When the boys were too exhausted to move, they were told to sit and listen. A rebel leader was their teacher. He was short, wore torn and soiled army clothes, and stomped around the clearing swearing and yelling. Perhaps he was twenty years old. Tony and the other students who had proven to be good soldiers sat right up front.

The teacher, if he could be called such a thing, held guns up in each hand and waved them like flags. He pointed out anti-tank mines, anti-personnel mines, and rocket launchers with red tails. The guns had English alphabet letters—SPGs, SMGs, B10s—and there were SAM7 missiles and RPGs, rocket-propelled grenades that could puncture armor. The boys learned to dismantle and assemble the guns and clean them, too. Their teacher finished the lessons by screaming, "You will obey your commander above all else. The very best soldiers are given many wives. If you prove yourself in battle, you too will be given many wives."

Wives? Who would want a wife?

Then came more threats, more yelling, but it was so hard to listen, so hard to stay awake, so thirsty, so hungry. At the end of each day—after walking, walking, walking, after lessons in guns and soldiering, and after prayers—Jacob, Paul, and Norman slumped down, too numb to speak. All the students of the George Jones Seminary were sickening for home. The cuts on their backs were healing but the itching was unbearable. They crumpled under a jackfruit tree. Norman's eyes rolled back in his head. "Norman, are you all right?" Jacob would ask again and again and Norman would nod over and over. Every day Norman seemed to grow smaller. Hope, he was losing hope. Jacob had to do something, anything, to make Norman and Paul think of something else.

But what?

Do not think about home. Do not think that the people who care for you are far away. How far? Hard to know. Think of something else entirely.

He had an idea. Jacob looked around. The soldiers were eating and paying them no mind. He motioned to Paul and Norman to come closer.

"Paul, tell us about America," whispered Jacob.

Norman perked up just a tiny bit and edged in still closer.

Paul's eyes widened in surprise. Then he shook his head. It was hard, too hard to think about that other life.

"Tell us about their clothes," Jacob egged him on. Paul thought for a minute, then said, "In America, many people wear strange things on their heads, hats of all kinds, caps too, some round and others made of wool, no matter what the temperature."

Jacob nodded. There were lots of books in the school library that were sent from people in America. One book was called *The Cat in the Hat*. Jacob looked up into the darkening sky and pictured white people all over America wearing tall, stripy hats.

"And they have every color of hair—yellow and orange and blue. Some of it sticks up in points. Many have long hair that curls."

Blue hair? Jacob almost laughed.

"Is everyone rich in America?" To Jacob's amazement, it was Norman who asked the question.

"I think so. Everyone uses electricity, even children are allowed to touch a switch on the wall. There is a lot of electricity. The ground is covered in cement and there are no cows. There are no animals anywhere! Except dogs. They walk dogs on the end of a rope and the dogs are made to wear clothes. And the little kids are impolite to their parents and they don't get beaten."

Both Jacob and Norman sucked in their breath. Imagine being rude to a parent and not being punished. But dogs wearing clothes! How could that be?

For a minute it worked. For a sliver of time their thoughts were elsewhere.

▪▪▪

Nyuma geuka. Left right, left right.

The rainy season arrived, slowly at first, droplets in the middle of the day. The drops turned to showers, the showers turned into storms, and color was brought into existence. And when the rain abated there were green mango trees standing under a yellow sun that shone down on the red earth.

The rain should have cooled their skin but it did not. It was hot, sticky water that evaporated in an instant. The ground became slippery scarlet rivers of muck. Mud caked their feet, ran up their legs, and splattered into their faces and eyes. Sitting in mud. Sleeping in mud. Mud for food. Mud for brains. Lightning threatened, thunder clapped, and the rain came down. They walked. Multiplying helped. Only in a civilized world did numbers mean anything.

89 times 99 equals 8,811.
66 times 97 equals 6,402.
Nyuma geuka. Left right, left right.

Jacob's shirt stuck to him like a crust. His shoes would not come off. His feet were so swollen that his ankles bulged and his toes curled under. The only way to remove his shoes easily would be to cut them off and—what then?

He looked down at Norman's bare feet. Gingerly, with his mouth clamped shut to hold in a cry, Jacob strained and yanked off his shoes. Jacob worked the shoes onto Norman's feet. They lasted a few days, then fell apart, leaving Norman barefoot again.

When he could, Jacob washed Norman's feet in muddy streams

and checked for infection. At least Norman didn't have chiggers—ticks—that burrowed into feet and ate up the foot from the inside out.

"Norman, can you feel this?" Jacob flicked the soles of Norman's feet with his fingers. Norman shook his head. Jacob made shoes for Norman out of banana leaves. He whispered as he wrapped the leaves around Norman's feet and tied them with vines, "Norman, what is 154 times 29?"

Norman shook his head.

"What is 12 times 10?"

"120," he whispered. "Good, that is good."

Paul was barefoot too. His shoes were now on the feet of a soldier.

95 times 78 equals 7,410. Maybe.

To pass the time, Jacob counted the number of soldiers and students in their unit. There were two hundred soldiers, slaves, and women in their group, including the thirty-seven students from George Jones. That number swelled and shrank. Sometimes they met up with other units of the LRA and more soldiers joined them.

Nyuma geuka. Left right, left right.

The only relief came at night.

"Did you hear?" A boy came out of the dark and squatted in front of Jacob and his friends. His name was Abraham, another student from their school. Abraham shuff led closer to Jacob and whispered, "Kony is nearby. They say that he will inspect the troops." Abraham was jubilant. He was beginning to turn, beginning to see a place for himself as a rebel soldier. It was starting to happen to many students. The lies told by the commanders were starting to take root. "We should pray that he comes to bless us." Abraham leapt up and went off to spread the gossip to the next group.

"What do you think Kony is like?" whispered Paul. There were rumors that Kony had magical powers, that he had thirty wives and two hundred children and lived like a king in the Sudan. Some said that he was three meters tall, while others said that he was powerfully built, with the body of a mighty warrior.

The next day came and went, and the day after that, and still Kony did not come.

13
ATTACK!

A scout came running back through the bush, eyes bulging, arms waving. He was nearly delirious with excitement. Although yelling was not allowed, no one seemed to care about his noise.

"What is it?" Paul, walking behind Norman, leaned forward. "I can't hear. What did he say?"

"He says that there is an unprotected village one day's march away. There must be plenty of food," hissed Jacob over his shoulder.

The news ran down the line like wind. Laughter followed in ripples. The excitement stopped the march.

Jacob doubled over. The pain in his stomach was getting worse every day and his kidneys ached. The sight of Norman and Paul close up took Jacob's breath away. Did he look as bad? Elbows and knees were like knotted ropes stuffed under peeling and dry reptilian skin. Cheekbones stood out in jagged ridges. Even their noses and earlobes were growing smaller. *Birds*, Jacob thought, *we look like bony birds*. He would sleep if he could, close his eyes and never wake up.

"Jacob?" Norman whispered. Jacob snapped his eyes open. Norman looked at him with concern. No, not concern, thought Jacob, fear. Jacob was Norman's lifeline, and maybe Paul's too. If Jacob showed any sign of weakness, Norman trembled.

There was a command to squat down. All the boys, girls, and children, too, tumbled onto the ground, grateful for a moment's rest.

Commander Opiro called a meeting of his lieutenants. Jacob spotted Oteka. They exchanged glances but nothing more. There was no opportunity to speak together.

Jacob strained to hear bits and pieces of the discussion. They seemed to be quibbling about what to do. One lieutenant said that the villagers might get wind of a rebel advance and run away with their supplies. Another said that the villagers had scouts too. They could be spotted at any moment.

"We must act now," said one of the lieutenants.

Commander Opiro made a decision. The strongest soldiers would race ahead and attack at first light. Opiro smiled at Lizard. Lizard would select the soldiers and lead the charge. Eddie would be his second-in-command. Lizard strutted down the line, a piece of bark between his teeth. "You, you, you …" He pointed to the fittest and the fastest boys and girls, all of whom squatted like schoolchildren waiting for the teacher to pick them. The girls, too, wanted to fight. To earn food to feed themselves—and the babies strapped to their backs—they had to go into battle just like boys.

Jacob, Paul, and Norman sat side by side and watched as Lizard came down the line, closer, closer. Hunger focused the mind, hunger made you mean, hunger made you forget everything except hunger.

"Only soldiers eat. If you want to eat, you will join us. This is your choice. If you die of hunger, it is your choice." The commander's words rolled around in Jacob's head. If only he could talk to Oteka.

Paul looked at Jacob. His eyes were wide and sad. Unless they had food they would die soon. Norman surely would; he was too weak to fight. But if Jacob and Paul joined the battle, they could share their food with him.

As Lizard came toward them, Jacob stood up. "Yes, I will go." There, he had done it. It was over. He would be a soldier now. Paul stood too.

Lizard looked over his shoulder toward Commander Opiro, then turned back. He laughed in Jacob's face. "You choose *now* to join us?" Lizard shook his head in disgust and walked away.

Jacob's heart pounded. Why did Lizard not want them to fight? But he had seen something, seen it distinctly. When Jacob asked to join, Lizard looked at Commander Opiro. Why? Something was wrong. The boys from George Jones were beaten, worked to near death, and starved, but, except for Adam, who had already been badly wounded, none had been murdered. Abducted children were either sent into battle immediately or forced to kill each other. That was always the case with the children taken from the villages. That was the rule. Those who would not fight were made an example of and killed. So, why had they been left alive? Why?

The selected soldiers got ready to leave. Oteka was chosen too. Jacob, Norman, Paul, and the rest were ordered to watch the ritual that would guarantee victory. Norman crept between Jacob and Paul, as if trying to crawl under protective wings.

The soldiers knelt down facing east and listened to a reading from a tattered, dog-eared Bible. "Behold, I will bring evil upon this people, even the fruit of their thoughts, because they have not hearkened unto my words, nor to my law, but have rejected it."

All repeated, "God is on our side."

Lizard and his second-in-command, Eddie, doused the rebel soldiers' heads with water to wash away their sins. Bottles of holy water were tied around their necks and magical stones looped around their wrists. They were ready to kill.

As the soldiers set out, Oteka looked back at Jacob. Their eyes met. Oteka seemed to be saying something to him, but what? And then he was gone.

Nyuma geuka. Left right, left right.

Without the presence of the commander or his lieutenants, the soldiers left to guard them slowed their pace. Not one of the soldiers was older than fifteen. Midday, they stopped. The soldiers propped their guns against a tree and ate something from a shared bag. No food or water was offered to the children, women, or slaves.

"Jacob," Paul hissed, and motioned to him to come closer. Jacob looked over his shoulder and then scurried, crab-like, toward Paul. Norman came too.

"Lizard did not want us. Why?" There was fear in Paul's eyes.

Jacob just shook his head. Paul, too, knew that they should be dead by now. Only Norman seemed oblivious to their situation.

"Do you know where we are?" Paul asked, and again Jacob shook his head. The land near the capital city, Kampala, was lush and forest-like. Plains and shrubs surrounded Gulu. But here, in this place, there was only bush, scrub, and thistle bushes that scraped their feet and legs. The sun told them their direction, but some days they walked north, other days south. There was talk that they had crossed into the Sudan. The Sudanese government supported Kony and the LRA. If they really were in the Sudan, the Ugandan government soldiers would not come after them. If they were in the Sudan, they were lost forever.

"Jacob, we could run away. Now, I mean. They would not come after us and leave the rest." Paul nodded toward the handful of boy–soldiers guarding them, two of whom were asleep.

Jacob pulled his knees up to his chest. To go off and wander aimlessly might deliver them into the hands of Sudanese soldiers, who would only return them to the LRA. And they could not expect help from villagers. Some might help but some would not. How to tell the difference? And if the LRA caught them, they would be killed, or worse. They would lose their arms or legs. He had seen the girl without ears many times. She walked alone, tall and elegant, one hand holding the bundle on her head, the other swaying in a gently melodic motion. She walked as if she was singing in her mind. She carried on her head as much as a mule and she carried it with grace.

Jacob had tried to speak to her one day when they had stopped to rest. He had told her his name, and asked what hers was.

"I know your name. Go." She'd shooed him away. "They will kill you if you are caught talking to a woman, even one like me." Timidly she had touched an ear, or the place where an ear had once been. But as he'd turned away she had whispered, "My name is Oyela Hannah."

Paul shook Jacob's arm. "Jacob, what is wrong? Are you listening? Now is our chance. Jacob, what should we do?" Jacob's mind wandered a lot lately. One thought would lead to another, and then he could not remember what he'd been thinking about in the first place.

"Jacob!" Paul nudged him.

Jacob pulled away. When had *he* become their leader? At school, Paul had been the brave one, the outgoing one, the leader. And Tony had been the good one, the boy everyone respected. Jacob had been the shy one. No one had bothered him. No one had even noticed him! How was he to know what to do? What was right? What if he got them killed? What if he had to watch them die? He was so tired. So hungry. So thirsty. Swallowing hurt. Talking hurt. He rubbed his throat constantly, trying to make it wet. Everything was blurred. Right and wrong had no edges, they folded in on themselves. But maybe Paul was right: if they were going to make a run for it, now would be the time. *Now.* Something was different—he was sure of it. Oteka had been trying to tell him something. And then an idea! Slowly his thoughts came together. What if government soldiers lay in wait in the village? What if the rebel soldiers were falling into a trap? Was that Oteka's message to him? "Jacob, what should we do?" Paul gave him another gentle nudge.

Jacob hugged his knees. He knew his thinking was erratic, but the more he thought about it, the more likely the idea became. *Government soldiers were waiting to ambush the LRA in the village ahead!* Of course, that's how a trap would be set and Oteka knew! The idea became more plausible with every passing second. The government soldiers knew the habits of the rebels, how they slaughtered, how they killed. Perhaps the entire village ahead was a fake! And then another idea: perhaps his father knew about it, perhaps his father was waiting in the village. At that moment, with hunger eating away at him, with his thoughts running wild, it made all the sense in the world. His father would rescue him.

"No, we stay," said Jacob firmly. He was very sure. If they stayed with the others, they would be led right to the village, to their rescue.

Norman looked to Paul. Sadly, in confusion, Paul shrugged.

The guards roused themselves. They were given the order to march.

Nyuma geuka. Left right, left right. They all tromped forward, one foot after the other. Soon, thought Jacob, soon he would be home. Walk. The pain in his feet melted away. He would be safe again. He would eat Bella's roasted chicken. He could almost taste it. He would never again complain about swallowing Ethel's foul medicines. Walk. Walk. Walk. Faster. Faster. Faster. They weren't far now. This time, Jacob was so sure, this time the rebels would be beaten. His walk turned into a jog. With every step the air grew thicker and hazier. In the distance black smoke twisted up into the blue sky like a python trying to reach Heaven. Guns went off, *pop-pop* and *rat-a-tat*. Hope soared.

"Jacob ... Jacob!" Norman cried.

Jacob began to run. He could almost fly. "They are here!" Jacob reached back and grabbed Norman's bony arm. "We are saved."

Norman pulled away. "What are you talking about?" Norman's eyes were wide and terror-filled. These were the first words he had uttered in many days, but Jacob didn't hear them. Jacob spun around and ran through the bush, thrashing with his arms.

"Come back. Come back!" Norman cried. He tried to keep up, he ran too and then, huffing, puffing, he fell to his knees.

"What is it? What's wrong? " Paul came up from behind.

Norman pointed down the path.

"What is he doing?" He didn't wait for an answer. Paul broke into a full run. With his long legs he soon caught up. Paul tackled Jacob and pinned him to the ground.

"What are you doing? You will get killed!"

"They're here. We have been rescued!"

Conviction outweighs strength every time. With all the force Jacob could muster he tossed Paul to the side, scrambled onto his feet, and bolted down the bush path toward the village.

Paul rolled over, spitting out dirt. He looked back. Rebel soldiers were taking aim at Jacob's back. Paul jumped up and spun around like a half-mad medicine man calling the spirits.

"Don't shoot. See, see, he is not running away. See, see, he is going *toward* the village. Don't shoot. He is going to fight. See, SEE!"

Jacob could smell the village before he could see it. Soured blood, smouldering ash, urine—the stink of killing went up the nose and stayed there. He came to the clearing in the middle of the village. Where were they? Where were the government soldiers? He twisted around and around like a leaf caught in a whirling wind.

Blood-drunk and sluggish, a group of rebels lounged by a small fire near a great *owii* tree, a holy tree. Sticky juice of different fruits—mango, watermelon, and pineapple—shone on their cheeks, noses, and chins. They looked at Jacob curiously. Lizard especially was taking notice.

Jacob spun around, mouth agape, eyes wide, huffing, puffing, trying to take in the scene around him. No government soldiers. No rescue. His body began to quake as tears raced down his face. He threw his hands up to the sky and screamed, *"Father, where are you? Why have you left me alone in this place? I am your son. Father, I need you."*

14
CEN—EVIL SPIRITS

Oteka did not appear to look up as he prepared food. Instead he seemed to busy himself with the chicken carcasses, *matooke* steaming in a pot over a fire alongside pancake bread and pots of vegetables. But he was watching. From a distance he took note of Jacob staggering around like a *lamero.*

"Angut!" Oteka cursed under his breath. Jacob was sobbing uncontrollably. Had the soldiers not had their fill of killing this day, Jacob would have been dead by now, no matter what Kony had ordered. It was Jacob's good fortune that their minds were on other things.

Behind Jacob came Paul. He raced into the village, his eyes darting in every direction. Paul spotted Oteka standing by a makeshift table near the fire. *Where is he? Where is Jacob?* Paul spoke with his eyes.

Oteka motioned with his head. *There,* he seemed to say. *He's over there.*

Norman followed, his eyes filled with fear. Then came the women, children, and slaves, all straggling into the village.

Oteka expertly drained the blood from the chickens, dipped the carcasses into hot water, then began the business of plucking the feathers. Several stringy chickens, giblets removed, were ready for the fire. Small children were gathered near him, all starving, all silently watching him. Girls looked at Oteka in wonder. Men did not cook, even if they were hungry.

Oteka flung two more chickens into the fire, then looked across the compound. Lizard was eating a mango. The skin of the fruit was held tight against his mouth, and juice dribbled down his chin. His small eyes were glued on Jacob.

"Angut!" Oteka repeated as he shook his head. The behavior of Jacob and his friends was dangerous. From the moment Oteka was captured he had watched, learned, and thought only of survival and escape. All else was forgotten. Forgetting was the key, something Jacob and his friends could not learn, or refused to learn. If Oteka thought of what it was to go to school, have parents and brothers and sisters, or make plans for the future, he knew he would go mad and behave as Jacob was behaving right at this minute.

Oteka looked down at the children who sat silently watching him, their eyes as round as coins, their mouths agape like little birds in a nest. He scanned the village quickly then flung uncooked strips of chicken skin toward the smaller children. They gobbled it down in seconds, leaving no greasy telltale signs.

While the chickens roasted over the fire a soldier held up a large wind-up radio and laughed. He turned a knob and the radio crackled to life. A cheer went up! Soldiers sitting farther away moved in close to hear the news. All the soldiers—the new ones and the older ones—and the girls and slaves, too, leaned in to listen.

Paul and Norman had managed to make Jacob sit still behind a hut. He was not completely out of sight, but it was the best they could do.

"Jacob, are you fine?" whispered Paul. Jacob nodded but did not look either boy in the eye. Slowly he was returning to himself. "Norman, stay with Jacob." As always, Paul spoke under his breath. "I will get closer and listen to the news on radio." Paul went off, while Norman, still trembling, snuggled closer to Jacob.

The radio sputtered and popped, shooting out words like electrical sparks. A deep, unwavering voice proclaimed the news of Kitgum and Gulu—who had taken a wife, who had given birth. The announcer read off the names of those who had died recently. Eddie, a tough soldier with slanted eyes, a flattened nose, and pale streaks across his cheeks, heard his father's name. His father was dead. Eddie put his scarred face in his hands and sobbed.

Then there was a message from the government for Kony. Jacob emerged from his fog and leaned forward. They were not terribly close to the radio but both boys could hear well enough.

The World Court in a place called The Hague had declared Kony a great enemy of the people. All the students of George Jones cocked their heads like confused dogs. What was a world court? How would this help them? Not one knew what a *hague* was, but many soldiers cheered anyway. Their leader was famous all over the world! And then the radio announcer said that there was a message for the students of the George Jones Seminary for Boys.

The students—and the soldiers, too—snapped to attention. There was a pronounced intake of breath all around. All the students looked like cats ready to pounce. Jacob looked around. Where was Tony? There, sitting near the fire, crouched down on his haunches and nestled up against his gun. *Listen, Tony, listen.*

"To the students of the George Jones Seminary for Boys, our prayers are with you," said the voice on the radio. Jacob's heart began to pound.

Then … nothing.

That was it? That was all? An involuntary sob seemed to spring from Norman's mouth as Jacob crumpled back to the ground.

The soldiers slapped their knees and laughed. Tony, trailing the butt of his gun in the dirt, walked toward Jacob and hovered above him. Jacob looked up at his friend's face. Tony was almost unrecognizable. Blue rings circled his eyes and his voice was low and raspy, not the sound of Tony at all. And when he spoke a white tongue was visible.

"You see? We are the enemy now," hissed Tony. "Our school—they do not want us back. You think that you can go home? You cannot. None of us can go home again. We have *cen* in us now—evil spirits." Tony's mouth curved into a sneer, although tears pooled in his eyes. "You think that if you do not kill they will take you back? They will not believe you. They will treat you like a murderer. Even your father. If you walk down a street they will run from you. They will put us all in jail and we will die there." Tony leaned down toward Jacob. His hands, his arms, and his legs quivered. "You are not a rich boy any longer. This is where we live now. We are rebel soldiers. We are LRA. We are killing for God, for the Acholi people, for Uganda. We have been forgotten."

Tony turned and walked away.

"Tony, no. Come back." Jacob called after him. But Tony did not turn around. Instead he walked toward the middle of the village. A soldier, sitting under the *owii* tree, passed Tony a bottle of soda stolen that day from the back of a truck. Tony popped off the cap with his teeth and sat.

"To the students of George Jones Seminary for Boys, our prayers are with you." Jacob mouthed the words then wiped his face, covered his ears with his hands, and nestled into the exposed roots of a sweet-smelling jackfruit tree. Nothing hurt as much as this, nothing. Not the beatings. Not the hunger. Not the thirst, or the pain of his rotting feet.

"Did you hear that?" Paul dropped down onto his knees. He was happy. Elated even. "What's wrong? Jacob, this is good news!"

Paul looked to Norman, who shrugged. "Did we hear what? We just heard that people are praying for us," said Norman.

Paul looked confused. "No, after that. Right after that. The announcer said that children who have been abducted into the rebel army need not fear arrest. Did you hear that, Jacob? Amnesty!" Paul crouched low. "The man on the radio said that if abducted children in Kony's army can get home, we will not be prosecuted. The soldiers will not shoot at us if we are unarmed. We can go home! Jacob, Jacob!" Paul looked confused.

Jacob said nothing, just stared at the ground.

"Do not give up, Jacob, do not." Paul looked around.

What to do?

Paul motioned to Norman to come closer, and then he whispered, "There is a river in New York called Hudson but no one goes to it with their buckets. Water comes out of taps in the wall. Many Americans live in apartments in the sky, many floors up. I do not know why they say *floors* when the apartments have walls and ceilings, too. And Jacob, there are thousands and thousands of buildings that rise as high as a plane flies, and the buildings are lit up with lights, day and night. They keep the electricity on when no one is around. Jacob? *Jacob?*"

Jacob mopped his face with the back of his hand. America? Could there be such a place? Jacob looked at Paul. He was trying so hard to be brave but he looked so scared. Norman looked worse. Norman's mouth quivered; his whole body trembled. Jacob had let them down. How could he have been such a fool?

"Norman, it's all right now. I am fine." Jacob tried to smile.

Eyes wide and hopeful, Norman nodded.

Jacob sighed. A truth had been building up inside him for a long time. And then, as with all revelations, it arrived in a flash. He looked from Norman to Paul and over to where Tony sat. The boys from the school were scattered about. He looked from one to the other. *No one was coming to save them.* His father could not save them. The government soldiers could not, or would not, save them. A certain resolve settled into his heart.

"We have to save ourselves," Jacob whispered. No one heard, not even Paul. *"We will save ourselves."*

15
HANNAH

Hannah would know things. She often cut up food for the commanders and served them too. She was ignored and therefore invisible, but she wasn't blind and she wasn't deaf. She would surely have information that could help save them … but would she talk to him?

It was Sunday, their only day of rest from constant walking and sporadic attacks on villages, trucks, buses, or people simply going about their business. Hannah sat behind a hut, legs tucked underneath her, hands together. From a distance it appeared as if she was praying; up close she looked as though she was someplace deep within herself, somewhere far away.

"For you." Jacob held out a piece of pancake bread that Oteka had passed to him at great risk. Hunger tore at Jacob's insides. It took all his self-restraint not to shove it into his mouth and gobble it down.

Bread! Hannah looked up at him, then around to see if they were being watched. Slowly she lifted her arm … then, fast as a gecko, grabbed the food out of his hand. "I have nothing for you. Why do you bring me food?" She ate quickly lest her good fortune be snatched back.

"I …" Jacob didn't know what to say. He didn't know how to talk to her, or to any girl, for that matter. He wanted to know about what the commanders were planning. But if he asked her outright, maybe she would think he was a spy. He had to try to become a friend. He *wanted* to be her friend, but how? She was prettier than he'd first thought. She had high cheekbones, a thin nose, and the eyes of a tiger, nut-brown with flecks of gold … dangerous eyes.

"Go." She motioned with her hand. "Sit over there and do not look at me. If anyone comes, pretend that you do not know I am here."

Jacob did as he was told. He crouched down on his haunches behind a hut and looked off into the distance. What now? If he were at home, in the back garden under the mango tree, what would he say?

"Where are you from?" he asked, politely.

Out of the corner of his eye he could see her shoulders pull back as if she was startled by the question. "I am from a village near Kitgum."

"I have been to Kitgum." In his mind's eye he saw red roads, little shops, painted buildings, a sweet place, like Gulu, but much smaller.

"What of your family?"

Hannah paused and seemed to consider her answer. "A curse was put on my father when I was ten years old, and he died. Then my mother died, too, but of tuberculosis. I had a sister but she ran away. The others—cousins, aunts, uncles—all gone."

"How were you … how did you come to …?" This was harder than he'd thought.

"The LRA were always raiding our village. They took away lots of boys and girls. I had a friend. Her name was Sarah. She was alone too, so we became sisters." Again she stopped.

They sat in silence for a while. Jacob waited. Should he say something? Ask another question?

"I find it difficult … it is that … speaking takes practice," Hannah stammered.

"I do not mean to …" said Jacob. But what did he mean? Hannah took a deep breath. Again she looked over his shoulder.

They both did. "The government representatives came to our village and said that we would be safer in a displacement camp. So Sarah and I left our village and moved into the camp. But the rebels broke into the camp and abducted many children. We were afraid. So then the government representatives said that if the children in the camp walked to Kitgum we would find protection there.

"At night we—I mean Sarah and I—walked from the camp to the refugee center in Kitgum. They called us night commuters. There were places for us to sleep—tents, wooden shelters, churchyards. But we were not safe, no one kept us safe. Bad boys bothered all the girls. Even the police and army soldiers bothered us. *Boda-boda* boys too. They ran around us with their little motorcycles as we were walking. They scared us. I want to become a sister, a nun. I thought that the nuns would not take me if a boy spoiled me."

Footsteps! Not heavy ones. Maybe a child. They waited in silence. Moments passed before Hannah spoke again.

"Some nights were very bad, and we had to stay awake to watch out for the boys who would bother us. One night Sarah and I decided not to walk to Kitgum. We stayed in the village, and that was the night the LRA came again. They killed many and then they took us away. Sarah was my family." Hannah stopped. Jacob stole a glance. She looked surprised, as though she couldn't believe she had talked so much.

Jacob did not ask about Sarah. He knew: however it had happened, Sarah was dead. Right then Jacob wanted to say that Hannah could be part of *his* family. Norman and Paul were his family, and maybe Tony too … even if Tony didn't care about them anymore. Hannah could join them, and even if they could not talk to each other freely or easily, she would *know* that she was part of a family.

"Your ears ..." He regretted the words immediately.

Hannah bolted up and forward, as if she had been hit hard on the back. "What? You think I suffer because they took off my ears?" She spat out the words. "The women say that I am cursed, and so they leave me alone. The men find me ugly and so the commander does not give me away as a co-wife. I will not be a co-wife. It is not the Christian way for one man to have many wives. The commander points to me, and then all the women are afraid and do what they are told. And even the soldiers do not want me to go into battle because they say that I will bring evil spirits down on them. But I am lucky and I am strong. I can carry more than *two* women. As long as I do not get sick, I will live and I will escape. One day."

"I am ..." He was sorry for asking such a question, but when he turned to face her, she was gone.

Fool, he thought. He had done this all wrong. He had found out nothing about the commanders, nothing about their location. Instead of befriending her he had offended her, and it might be weeks before he had such an opportunity to speak with her again. He had failed. Jacob sat in the dark for a long time and listened to the frogs and the crickets and bush babies whining, thinking over what had happened. Perhaps, he decided, he had not failed completely. Now he knew that Hannah wanted to escape, too. He knew something else: she was brave and smart.

There was no plan in Jacob's head, not yet, but from here on he would be ever vigilant. As his body grew weaker, his mind grew stronger.

There were *some* questions he knew the answer to. Why were they always walking? Oteka had said it was to hide from the government soldiers and to find food. That, in Jacob's experience, was true.

How many soldiers were in Kony's army? How could anyone

tell? With the boys from the school there were about two hundred in this brigade, and Oteka had said there were four brigades. Did that mean that Kony had eight hundred soldiers? Maybe not.

They marched in a straight line, following in each other's footsteps. Why? Perhaps because that would make it hard for the government army to estimate their number. They slept in long grass, because even though they flattened it in the night, it would take its shape again under the noonday sun and hide all traces. Again, this would make it hard for the government soldiers to estimate their numbers. He was beginning to see a pattern, a method to the madness of the LRA.

Jacob would make mental notes concerning the comings and goings of the commanders. He had a good memory. Commander Opiro was away most of the time. The truck that carried him off like a king did not always bring him back the same day. It was said that he was in meetings with Kony. It was said that there was a big plan to bring all four brigades together and attack Gulu, or maybe Kitgum. It was also said that some nights Opiro and other commanders drove into Gulu and had dinner at a hotel. Why were they not arrested? Did people not know who they were? Father sometimes ate at the hotel in Gulu. That night, Jacob watched as Commander Opiro climbed into the truck with loppy tires and drove away. He left Lizard in charge. Lizard now carried a cellphone. And he had a new title: Lieutenant Lizard.

16
LITTLE GIRLS

"There is a convoy of government soldiers coming our way." Lizard snapped his cellphone shut and rammed it in his pocket. The phone was a badge of authority, proof that he was in command. "Who will volunteer to fight?"

Once again, hands shot up. Jacob, Paul, and Norman just sat on their haunches, secure in the knowledge that they would be passed over.

"You—do you fight today?" Lizard looked down at the three and grinned.

Startled, Jacob and Paul leapt up. Yes! Food, they wanted food.

Lizard laughed and nodded. "Give them *pangas*," he yelled.

Both boys took the long knives. Norman looked on.

He was not given a *panga*.

Preparation for battle began. The soldiers knelt down, facing east. Lizard retrieved a damaged prayer book from a pocket.

"Saint Michael, Archangel, defend us in battle. Be our defence against the wickedness and snares of the devil. May God rebuke him, we humbly pray. And you, Prince of the Heavenly Host, by the power of God, thrust into Hell Satan and the other evil spirits who prowl the world for the ruin of souls. Amen."

In chorus they all responded, "God is on our side."

Lizard and his second-in-command, Eddie, dribbled water over their heads to wash away their sins. Now Jacob would kill—and perhaps die—but if he lived, he would eat. And if he ate, so would Norman. He dreamed of food; they all did.

The main group of girls, their children, and slaves were left behind in the tall grass as Jacob, Paul, and the rest went off to do battle.

They lay in two ditches beside the road, one ditch directly behind the other. Jacob and Paul, and many boys from their school, hid in the second ditch, *pangas* clutched to their sides. The rebel soldiers, including Tony, were in the forward ditch, the one closest to the road. They carried guns.

Lieutenant Lizard was poised to give the signal, his bloodshot eyes focused on the road. Jacob's heart thumped in his chest. He fingered the stones sewn into the tiny cloth bag that dangled from his wrist, magical stones that had the power to protect him from bullets. His fingers curled around the *panga*. He had gripped it so long and so hard that his hand hurt. All his muscles hurt. Everything hurt.

They waited, heads down. Then, a *pop*, *pop*, *pop*. Not the *rat-a-tat* of a big gun but the little sound of a little gun. A rebel soldier hiding down the road had shot out one of the truck's tires. In a flash of memory he thought of grasshoppers in a pot in Bella's kitchen. *Pop*, *pop*, *pop* was the sound they made as they tried to escape the inevitable.

Lizard held his hand up in the air. *Wait. Wait.* The open- backed truck veered all over the road before coming to a stop and tipping to one side. And then, "Attack!" The first wave of rebel soldiers surged out of the ditch, guns trained. Tony whooped the loudest.

"Attack!"

Lizard, Eddie, Tony, and the rest swooped down on the truck like great birds of prey. They pointed their guns but did not fire.

Lizard shouted the command again. "Attack!" The second wave rose up out of the ditch.

Jacob turned and looked Paul in the eyes. All they had to do was stand, raise their *pangas*, and kill. Then it would be over. Then they would be rebels. Then they would eat.

"Attack!"

Jacob felt his body lurch forward. He scrambled up and out of the ditch. He ran. His arms and legs seemed to spin but his brain stood still. And then he stopped, suddenly. He stood on the sandy road with his *panga* held over his head. Paul slammed into the back of him.

These weren't government soldiers.

These were children.

A dozen children and a few mothers sat on wooden benches in the back of the truck. They were on their way to school. The students wore blue tunics over pink shirts, and their book bags were flung over their shoulders. The children cried out at the sight of the soldiers bearing guns and knives. The mothers screamed.

Again Lizard shouted, "Attack!"

Jacob felt his body jolt forward. "Arrggghhh," he cried. Over and over. "Arrggghh." It was a guttural sound that came from a place deep within.

All around him the rebels rushed toward the truck, screaming, screaming, screaming. The high-pitched shrieks filled his ears and the air around him.

A little girl in the back of the truck clung to her mama. The mama poured her body over her child, cupping her in her bulk. Two rebel soldiers tried to peel the mama off. The mama hung onto her daughter's arms, then she seized the hem of the girl's school uniform, and as the material was ripped from her grasp she grabbed onto the girl's legs.

"Let her go! My baby, my baby!" she shrieked.

Jacob held his *panga* in the air, his face blank. The mama was strong. The muscles in her arms bulged and the veins in her neck swelled. He froze. The mama's shrill squeals stung.

Kill! Kill!

And then it came to him, a voice jumped into his head:

"Pussycat, pussycat, where have you been?"

In that moment, Jacob's world stood still.

Lizard sprang up onto the truck, knocked Jacob aside, then reared up and smashed the mama's teeth with his rifle butt. Still, the mama gripped her child's feet. Jacob wanted to shout at her, *Let go. Let go. It's too late. Your girl is lost!* But nothing came out of his mouth. The butt of Lizard's gun came down on her head a second time. She fell sideways. And then it was over, all of it.

Jacob stood on the road. His hands shook. His knees nearly buckled. He staggered to the edge of the road and heaved and retched until his whole body quivered with the effort. What had he heard? *Mother?* It was his mother's voice that had stopped him from killing. No, he was hungry, that was all. He was starving. He was imagining things. *But dead is not dead. Spirits do not die. If they love you, they stay and protect you.*

He looked up and saw Paul slumped in the ditch. Paul's *panga* lay on the ground beside him. There was no blood on the knife. For a moment, however brief, Jacob felt relief. But they had not killed, so they would not eat.

Three girls were abducted. The youngest was ten, maybe eleven, the oldest perhaps thirteen years old.

Under the cool, clear sky with hardly a cloud in sight, Jacob counted eight bodies on the road: two old women, an old man, the rest were mothers with babies. Not a single shot had been fired.

Paul hauled away crates of live chickens, while Jacob sifted through the belongings of the dead. Inside pockets or strewn in the dirt they uncovered a few coins, plastic water bottles, a basket of bananas, and a book on mathematics. It must have come out of a book bag. A soldier made off with the bananas while Jacob fingered the pages of the book.

"What is it?" Lizard had a habit of disappearing and reappearing. He could be in two places at one time, Jacob was sure of it. He was the devil, a wizard. If such things existed, then Lizard was one.

Lizard knocked Jacob back into the dirt. "What have you there?" He snatched up the book. "Arithmetic! You still think this matters? Killing is what matters! Being a good soldier matters. Making Kony proud matters." He threw the book on the ground, then stomped away in disgust.

Jacob picked up the book and dusted off the cover.

67 times 80.

He could not remember the last time he had tried to visualize numbers or multiply in his head.

67 times 80. It should have been so easy.

He said it out loud: *"67 times 80."*

He didn't know the answer. He couldn't *see* the numbers anymore.

Lizard was shouting. Jacob threw the book away and picked up his *panga*. He hoisted the last crate of chickens up on his head and began to walk back to camp. Rebel soldiers had tied the little girls up with tree vines, wrist to wrist. They were crying.

Back at camp the little girls, still tethered, huddled together. The older soldiers preferred to marry the very little girls and make them wives. The small ones had no hatching chiggers between their toes and no *twoo jonyo* AIDS between their legs.

As the chickens were being cooked over an open fire, Jacob

pulled his legs up to his chest. Tony strutted past Jacob, a bloody, pink chicken leg in his hand. Tony was now a respected soldier.

"Tony?" Jacob whispered his name. Tony ignored him.

It was late in the day, time to rest if not to eat. Jacob folded his arms across his knees and let his head loll back and forth. What had Lizard read out of the prayer book, about Saint Michael, the Archangel?

"Michael, Archangel, defend us in battle. Be our defence against the wickedness and snares of the devil." Where had he heard that before? Church, maybe? School?

"Come, eat." Paul pulled at Jacob's arm.

"But I didn't kill anyone," Jacob said.

"I did not kill either. Never mind. We have to *try* and eat." Paul pulled Jacob's arm again.

Slowly Jacob got up on his feet. Norman, silently, stumbled behind. Norman seemed to be growing backwards, shrinking, getting smaller and smaller.

As usual Oteka stood by the fire. Without looking at the boys directly, he handed them three big pieces of meat. They shoved the meat into their mouths. Streams of fat rolled down their chins. The chicken was stringy, tough, pink, and delicious.

"Stop! You did not kill today!" Lizard pushed Jacob aside, grabbed the hunk of chicken out of Norman's hand, then turned and stared at Oteka. His pea-sized eyes narrowed. It was apparent to all watching that Lizard was beginning to distrust Oteka. He flung the chicken into the dirt. A group of children pounced on it like small animals.

"You do not kill, you do not eat." With one hand Lizard rammed the nub of his gun barrel under Norman's chin, and with the other he grabbed him by the arm, spun him around, and sent him sprawling into the dirt. The few bites Norman had managed to cram into his mouth shot out in a spurt. Some soldiers laughed, others applauded. It was one less mouth to feed, all the more for them. Lizard raised the butt of his gun up and made ready to smash it into Norman's face. Norman held up his hands and cried out.

Jacob lurched forward. *Wait, I did not kill today either.* The voices in Jacob's head screamed and screamed—*No, no, no!*—but his feet were rooted to the ground.

A rumble—deep, menacing, distant—circled the village. It came from all directions at once. There was a pause, a collective drawing of breath. With the gun poised above Norman's head, Lizard stopped and sniffed the air like a rodent. A shout went up. Then they heard the trucks, dozens of them.

"Kony! He's here!"

17
KONY

A half dozen jeeps and trucks nosed through the bush while three or four more vehicles roared toward them from different directions on rutted paths. Dozens of motorcycles followed, spinning their wheels and kicking up dust before coming to a sliding stop. The engines strained and whined, some sounding like wounded animals, others like thunder rolling across the savannah.

The commanders stepped out of the trucks and Jeeps like celebrated, important men.

Paul sidled up close to Jacob. "They dress in white, like priests," he hissed in his ear.

Jacob nodded. These *priests*, these lords of the movement, looked very well-fed.

The commanders blustered and preened, swaying and swaggering in front of the starving children and young soldiers. One was small and dapper, the second was fat, and the third was a fit, tall man with a moustache that curled at the tips. He looked like a friendly grandfather, a *kwaro*. Commander Opiro, too, stepped down from the back of a Jeep. Immediately, Lizard and Eddie were at his side.

The soldiers and girls with babies clapped and cheered. Jacob, Paul, and Norman watched, caught in a whirlwind of confusion. Other students from the school seemed to cluster together. Their eyes asked: *What is this? What is happening?*

More and more rebel soldiers emerged from the bush. They materialized like dirty, wasted ghosts—dead eyes, moronic smiles. *Gemo*, thought Jacob, evil spirits who ushered in death.

They kept coming! Hundreds more soldiers poured into the village. Everyone was running. Old jerry cans of water were unloaded from broken-down trucks. The water was sprinkled on the ground. "Praise the Lord!" Blessings were cried out. Tables and plastic folding chairs appeared. Tents went up.

"Kony, Kony, Kony." The women whispered his name. "Kony, Kony." The name escalated into a cry. "Kony! Kony! Kony!" they screamed.

And then it all stopped. An eerie silence settled over the camp as they listened to the roar of an engine coming down a path.

Kony—*tipu*, prophet, holy one—arrived in a big Jeep, the biggest Jacob had ever seen. Cheers went up. Everyone was clapping. Jacob and Paul and all the boys from school stood silently, mesmerized by the spectacle. Norman, trembling, stood behind Jacob, desperately trying to hide.

Kony held up his hands, smiled, and accepted his due as their great leader. He stepped out of the Jeep and flopped down into a plastic chair under the holy tree.

Jacob gasped. *This was Kony?*

He was old, at least old to Jacob—maybe forty. He looked ordinary and small. Like the rest of the commanders he wore a long, white, pristine robe, and hanging around his neck was a large, gold, jewel-studded crucifix. But it did not make him look regal and strong. He looked like a cow wearing a cowbell. Fingering a rosary, Kony gazed over the crowd. Dark aviator glasses concealed his eyes, combat boots peeked out from under his robe, and dreadlocks dusted his shoulders.

A hiss ran through the crowd. "Lay down your guns. Remove your shoes." Guns were piled in heaps, although the soldiers who actually had shoes sat on them instead of giving them up.

Common soldiers sat on the ground, slaves and women behind. Only high-ranking soldiers sat on rickety plastic chairs around the holy tree. Where had all these soldiers come from? There were hundreds and hundreds of them. As Jacob looked over the crowd, a thought came from nowhere. Perhaps Musa Henry Torac's grandson was here. Michael, he was sure the boy's name was Michael. How would he find him? Likely the boy was dead, anyway.

"What do you think is going on?" Paul asked. Jacob just shook his head.

As more rebel soldiers spilled out of the bush and squatted on the ground, girls and their children formed a line next to Kony. Jacob, Paul, and Norman followed the others and sat.

One by one the girls presented their babies to their great leader. The infants were smeared with nut butter and ash, a mixture that promised to protect babies from bullets. Kony seemed to gaze at each one with mild amusement, but after the twentieth infant was held up for his inspection, boredom set in. With a regal flourish he waved the rest away.

A dead leopard was tied upside down to a pole. Its crimson tongue dangled out of a blood-encrusted mouth. The soldiers at each end of the pole paraded the dead cat around camp like a trophy heralding a great event. Jacob, Paul, and Norman stared at the dead animal. Its spotted black-and-gold hide shimmered. Hardly anyone had ever seen such a beast, and yet there it was. Where had it come from? In Uganda leopards lived only on the game reserves. Kony inspected the dead cat and after all had had a chance to marvel at it, the cat was taken off to be skinned.

"There will be a great feast," whispered Abraham, from school. He was always popping up with bits of gossip or news. He held his gun with pride. Abraham was now a soldier.

Prayers were announced. Everyone faced east, kneeled, and put their foreheads to the ground. *God would protect them. God was on their side. Father, Son, and Holy Spirit.*

Once the prayers were done and more blessings pronounced, a small, neat little man stood up and began talking. He was not introduced, no one was, but his name was hissed from person to person. He was Brigadier-General Vincent Otti, Kony's right-hand man. His white robe was immaculate, his hair carefully combed.

"He's very smart." Oteka squatted down behind Jacob. "He flew planes. He was an engineer in Israel and Russia." Jacob looked up in astonishment. How could such a man, who had travelled so far, end up here?

Brigadier-General Otti finished speaking, and the applause and cheers began again.

"We must talk—tonight," Oteka whispered into Jacob's ear. Without turning to look at Oteka directly, Jacob nodded. Oteka did not so much stand and leave as silently fade into the crowd, a hard thing for such a tall boy to do.

Kony stood and removed his aviator glasses. He took his time. Dipping his fingers into a bowl of water, he made the sign of the cross over the heads of the crowd. There was a hush, and then he began to speak.

"We are to fight the evil Museveni, who calls himself the president of Uganda. We know that Museveni wants to kill all the Acholi people. We must kill him first. We are here to fight and make a homeland for the Acholi people." His voice seemed to cast a spell over the crowd. It was said that God spoke through Kony, and that was why he could speak so well.

"We must learn the laws of the Bible and obey them. Isaiah says, 'And they that forsake the Lord shall be consumed.' We will consume our enemies and do God's work. Learn the Bible and know what it is teaching. David is killing Goliath with a holy stone. God wrote down this story for us. God is telling us that Museveni is Goliath. God is telling us that we can kill Museveni, and the soldiers he sends to attack us. God says we can kill Museveni's army with stones."

In one moment he spoke in a whisper and the next a bellowing cry. And then, when it seemed that he could not yell any louder, Kony's voice rose into a high-pitched wail. His eyes grew big and round and his hands flew up into the air. "God is telling us that killing is right. God wants us to kill and we will do as God tells us. We are soldiers of the Cross." His voice rang out through the bush, up, up, so that the animals in the trees, the birds in the air, and God Himself could hear. With arms reaching up to Heaven Kony cried, "God hear us and let blessings fall from the sky like sweet rain."

Tears of joy ran down the cheeks of the girls. Guns were fired into the air. Clapping and singing began as Kony looked down at his flock and made the sign of the cross. The dancing began. They laughed and clapped. Jacob and Paul too.

"Norman, dance," Jacob hissed in the boy's ear. Norman made a poor attempt to lift his heavy feet and bang his hands together.

This was madness, all madness. How could these girls be happy? Why were the boys cheering? *Why?* Kony had said, "God wants us to kill and we will do as God tells us." It was getting harder and harder for Jacob to separate the God of the Catholic Church and this God, the killing God, Kony's God.

Twice Jacob spotted Hannah peeking out from behind a hut. She was not cheering or clapping, and there were no tears of joy on her cheeks. If anyone had noticed her they would have seen contempt for Kony written on her face, but no one cared to look.

The leopard was roasted and eaten, along with more food than any of them had seen in months. They ate mashed *matooke*, millet porridge, and *kisra* pancakes, along with *do-do* and vegetables of all kinds. Even the children ate, vomited, and tried to eat again.

"Do not eat too much," Jacob hissed in his friends' ears. Already, the food they had consumed sat rock-hard in their guts.

Kony and his commanders met under a tent, the flaps pulled back so that all could see the great men in discussion. Jacob watched. Perhaps this was why Kony had come, to meet his men, to plan the great attack everyone talked about.

Darkness fell. As quickly as it had materialized, the great celebration was over. Trucks revved up. Many left the camp.

"What's happening?" asked Paul.

"It looks like they are leaving. Most of them, anyway," answered Jacob. It was unlikely that Kony would remain in camp overnight. It was said that he moved through the bush like a spirit and never stayed anywhere too long. Kony had much to fear. It was not only the government that wanted Kony dead. He had many enemies. Evil men always did.

The commanders and lieutenants—Lizard, Eddie, and Tony among them—could still be heard drinking soda and laughing across the village. Alcohol was forbidden. There was another sound too.

"Nooo-nya mwa-na wa-nge, nooo-nya mwa-na wa-nge."

"Singing! A girl is singing!" Paul slumped back on his haunches and shook his head in amazement. Jacob and Norman hunched down and closed their eyes, but the song kept calling them back from sleep.

"Nooo-nya mwa-na wa-nge, nooo-nya mwa-na wa-nge."

The girl's voice was high and fragile. Maybe she was one of the schoolgirls they had snatched off the truck.

"Looking for my darling, looking for my darling.

Nooo-nya mwa-na wa-nge, nooo-nya mwa-na wa-nge."

Norman curled up a few meters away and closed his eyes. He found peace in sleep. Jacob looked up at the moon. It was the same moon that was shining down on his father, the same moon that Paul had seen in America. Did anyone think of them? Did anyone know that they needed help?

Jacob looked over at Paul. The soles of his feet were thick with mud. But in the moonlight, when every tree, branch, and rock had turned the color of a shadow, Paul clasped his hands over his ears and slept. Jacob closed his eyes.

"Where is he?" Lizard stood above him, his gun jammed against Jacob's temple. Jacob jolted forward.

"Who?" asked Jacob, his throat constricted, his body suddenly rigid.

"Jacob?" Norman's voice drifted through the dark on a wave of fear.

Lizard spun around. "There you are. Get up. Did you think you would get away with stealing? Did you think you could eat the food meant for soldiers? Did you think I would forget? GET UP!"

"No, leave him alone." Jacob jumped to his feet. This time he would not back down. Never again.

Even in the dark one could almost feel Lizard sneer. "Do you think you are brave? You are stupid." Two other soldiers emerged from the dark. They pointed their guns, not at Jacob but at Paul, who now stood behind him. "Which friend do you want dead?"

Jacob fell silent as Lizard laughed.

They marched Norman away. The boy had not cried out, not said a word. Jacob sat down on the ground and put his head in his hands.

18
NORMAN WILL DIE

Oteka crouched down, placed his hand on Jacob's shoulder, and gently gave him a nudge. "They will kill your friend tomorrow."

Jacob was not asleep. In the distance he could hear men laughing. Paul had lain back down on the ground, but Jacob thought he might be only pretending to sleep. "Who will be killed?" Jacob asked, but he already knew that it was Norman. He absolutely knew.

"The little one. They will make you kill him. But you will all be dead soon." Oteka's whispers were so low that Jacob had to sit up and lean in to hear.

"How do you know such a thing?" asked Jacob. His voice was even, devoid of panic. Strangely, he felt a sort of relief wash over him. The moment had come.

"Did you hear the message to the boys from your school on the radio?"

"Yes," Jacob nodded. "It was, 'God bless.'"

"It was more than that. It was code. It said, 'The deal will not be completed.' I have listened to the commanders talk. Cooks hear many things. Kony was trying to negotiate with the parents of the boys in your school. Your father is head of the parents' group. Kony wanted guns in exchange for all of you. That is why Kony and Commander Opiro did not want you to go into battle. That is why your lives have been spared, until now." As he spoke, Oteka kept watch for any movement around him.

It made sense, all of it. The boys from the school had been treated in a way that was wrong according to the rules of the rebels. But that was why—they had been spared because they were to be *traded*. Even the boys from school who had become soldiers did not go into real battle with government soldiers. They attacked villages, or, thought Jacob, trucks filled with defenceless mothers and children. They were never put in real danger.

"What has gone wrong?" Jacob asked.

"The government stepped in and said that they would not allow the exchange of guns for the students. Everything was arranged—even the pickup of the guns. That is why Kony is so angry. All the brigades had come together to make a big attack. Without the guns, there will be no attack. That is why you are in so much danger. Since there is no arrangement, you are no longer of any use. It has been decided that those students who have not become good soldiers will be killed. Your friend Norman, he will be made an example."

Just like Adam, thought Jacob. He gazed up at the trees; still dark. He felt peaceful. Never mind death. His father had not forgotten him. To die and think that he had been forgotten would have been the worst death of all. Whatever fate awaited them, it was time to go out and meet it.

"You and your friend must escape tonight," Oteka whispered.

Which friend? He had *two* friends. But there was another more pressing matter. "Do you know where we are?"

"Yes, we are in the park. Murchison Falls, the safari park. I overheard one of the commanders say that we are east of Lake Albert."

The leopard … of course. That meant that they were only a hundred kilometers away from Gulu. Not in the Sudan, not lost.

"Why has Kony come so close to the government soldiers? Why has Kony taken such a risk?" To Jacob, this made no sense.

"Tourists come to the park, lots of them, and they pay a lot. If there is any trouble here the tourists will stop coming and the government will lose big money. The government wants no trouble in this area. They will not fire on the rebels here," whispered Oteka.

"Do you know this reserve?" asked Jacob.

"It's the biggest park in Uganda but I know it a little," whispered Paul. He had been listening. Paul crawled over now and hunched down between Oteka and Jacob. All three boys looked over their shoulders to see if anyone else was near.

"My father brought me to the park once. I know where Sambiya Lodge is," Paul told them.

"You must leave now. I am guarding a path that will take you toward the river. I will guide you to the edge of the village." Oteka stood and slung his gun from one shoulder to the other.

Jacob stood too and gently touched Oteka's arm. "Lizard suspects something. You are in danger. Come with us."

Oteka looked off into the dark, then up at the moon. It was a full moon. Not a good night to run away. And escaping as a group was especially dangerous. There were many soldiers in the camp, many guns, motorcycles, and trucks. Could such a crowd work in their favor? There would be a commotion at dawn, and it might be hours before they were missed, precious hours. Oteka had been biding his time, waiting for a sign from Adaa, from his parents, or from God. But what Jacob had said about Lizard was true. Lizard was young, and yet he was gaining power and favor with the commanders. He was especially dangerous, especially violent.

A cloud passed over the moon.

"It is greedy, this night," said Oteka. "I will come."

"If we are on the right side of the lake then the lodge is only ten, maybe fifteen kilometers away." Paul sounded so sure of himself that neither Oteka nor Jacob questioned him.

"And if we are on the wrong side of the river?" Jacob asked.

Paul shook his head. The river was filled with Nile crocodiles, some as long as six meters and capable of eating a lion or a human whole. And just as dangerous were the enormous, lumbering hippopotami who fed at night and just before dawn. The whole river came alive at night. If they were on the wrong side of the river, they would have more to worry about than the LRA.

"We must go. Follow me." Oteka took the lead.

Jacob was ready; he had been ready all along. "You two go on, I will catch up."

Instantly, without being told, Oteka knew what Jacob must be thinking. "Your friend Norman is lost. If we are to go, it is now," he hissed.

"Paul, go with Oteka. I will find Norman. We will follow."

Jacob's words were brave. He felt brave. There was nothing left *but* bravery. And he was thinking of Hannah. There had to be a way to reach her, to ask her to join them.

"No, *I* will find him," said Oteka. He did not know Norman as Paul and Jacob did, but he understood loyalty. And besides, he carried a gun. He was the cook and had never actually gone into battle, but the commanders valued him and so he was accepted as an LRA soldier. He could stride through the camp without arousing suspicion.

Oteka did not wait for Jacob to protest but set out at once. Jacob wanted to cry out, to tell him, *No, this is my decision*, but any noise would have put them all in danger.

Paul and Jacob crouched down on their haunches and waited. Frogs' croaking, crickets' chirping, the piercing cries of bush babies, and the drone of African music pouring out of wind-up radios filled the night. They waited. It seemed like a very long time.

Oteka finally reappeared and fell to his knees in front of them. His breath was short.

"He is in one of the commanders' tents. It is being guarded. There is no way we can rescue him. Kony has left, but there are over four hundred soldiers still in camp." Oteka ran his hand over his close-cropped hair.

"I have to try," whispered Jacob. They had survived this long because they cared about each other, a simple survival technique. But this was no suicide mission. He did not mean to die now. This new Jacob was not shy any longer. He was not a leader, not a follower either, nor was he a warrior. He was something else. He was his own person, and he was not afraid. God willing, he would fight to live, but never would he live to fight.

Oteka did not even try to reason with Jacob. It was obvious that Jacob would have to see the situation for himself. "Walk beside me, shoulders back. Carry your *pangas*."

Oteka gave the commands.

Heads high, shoulders squared, Jacob, Paul, and Oteka did their best to strut through the dark camp. They passed soldiers sprawling languidly around small fires, looking like corpses scattered carelessly by a small god. In the distance they saw the outline of an open tent lit from within by a kerosene lamp and heard a radio playing softly. The flaps of the tent were up. Four commanders sat on plastic chairs around a large plastic table. These loud, gruff, and crude men were in full view. The table and the ground around them were littered with soda pop bottles.

Oteka ducked behind a hut and motioned to Jacob and Paul to do the same.

Over there. Oteka mouthed the words and pointed to the canvas tent. There were four huts between the boys and the tent. A guard, chewing a stick and gripping an AK-47, crouched in front of it. The commanders, including the one with the moustache, sat not three meters away from the tent Norman was imprisoned in. Oteka was right: there was no way past the commanders and the guard.

Then Jacob saw her, or rather the outline of her— Hannah.

Clutching a small knife, Hannah stood in front of a makeshift plastic table slicing fruit. Carefully and artistically she placed the fruit slices on banana leaves. Jacob sniffed. He could smell meat too, goat and beef. With downcast eyes he watched her walk over to the open tent and serve the commanders. Her work went unacknowledged. A scarf, the one she usually wore around her head, was wrapped around her waist, like a belt. It was as if she wanted them to see her scars. She was right. She was beautiful but they did not notice. The scars protected her.

Jacob's hand scratched the dirt. He needed something to throw. No, that would be too obvious. How could he attract her attention? Jacob motioned to Oteka and Paul with a flat palm to wait. Crawling on all fours, he circled behind the huts, then finally, in a mad dash, rolled behind the tent. Norman was behind the canvas wall, possibly inches away, yet Jacob had no way of telling him that he was near.

The guard at the front of the tent was a meter away, maybe less. Jacob lay down in the dust and inched his way around the side of the tent. The powdery soil went up his nose. He stifled a sneeze. In this position, if he reached out with his right hand and really stretched, he'd touch the guard's foot. Chin on the ground, he watched.

One minute Hannah was in the pool of light cast by the lamp on the table, the next she was in the shadows. Twice she almost brushed against Jacob. The third time, as she swooped past, he reached out and gently, like a wisp of wind, touched her leg. Assuming an insect had grazed her leg, Hannah leaned forward to sweep it off. If his thoughts could have spoken to her, Jacob would have been crying out, *It's me, it's me!* He grabbed her hand, squeezed quickly, then let go. Everything—all their lives—depended on Hannah's not screaming out, not reacting in any way. He waited. Heart thumping in his ears. Mouth dry.

Nothing. She did nothing. And then a mango fell to the ground. Hannah reached down to retrieve it and looked into Jacob's eyes.

Jacob pointed, then scurried back into the darkness. Unblinking, undaunted, Hannah cut up more food, this time boiled pumpkin and okra, and again placed the tray of food in front of the commanders. Casually, arms swaying at her sides and head held high, she turned, picked up an empty jerry can, and walked back into the night.

They met behind a hut—Oteka, Paul, Jacob, and now Hannah. "Your friend, I have seen him. He is alive," whispered Hannah. She did not need to be told why they were there, she knew. Besides, there was no time for explanations.

"We must get him out," hissed Jacob.

Hannah shook her head. "There are too many commanders, and the guard …"

Rage rose up suddenly in Jacob. He'd had enough of being told what he could and could not do. He was not angry at any of them—his fury was for a world that would allow this to happen to them, a world that did not care enough to stop it from happening.

"I will not leave him."

They sat in silence for a moment, then Oteka said, "We will cut through the back of the tent."

"The noise?" said Hannah. The rip of a *panga* slicing through canvas would be heard by all.

"Can you turn up the radio?" Jacob lurched forward.

Ideas, they needed ideas. That and bravery. "Not without being told to do so."

Hannah faltered. She looked at the faces around her—Jacob, Oteka, Paul—and it was as though she began to draw strength from their courage emanating from them and enveloping her. She could be courageous too. She did not want to die but she would not fear death any longer.

"Yes, I can turn up the radio."

Jacob reached out and touched her hand. They both knew that she could be beaten for this, or much worse.

"Come with us. Escape," whispered Jacob. Oteka and Paul nodded.

Yes, she mouthed the word looking from one boy to another. She didn't need to think about it. *Yes. Yes. Yes.*

Jacob held Hannah's hand. Oteka laid his hand on top of Jacob's and Paul's on top of his. "Family," Jacob whispered. They all nodded.

There was a sound, a footstep. Motioning silently with their hands, they made plans. Oteka and Paul would walk back across the village and wait by the unguarded exit into the bush—unguarded because Oteka himself was supposed to be guarding it. Hannah would refill the jug, place it on the table, then "accidentally" knock over the radio. When she picked it up she would turn up the volume. Jacob would wait until the radio blared. He would have one chance to make a clean, long cut with a *panga* into the thick canvas. There was no way to warn Norman. If he was sitting too close to the tent wall, Jacob's *panga* would slice him in half.

Jacob leaned closer to Paul and whispered into his ear. "If we do not make it, tell them about us. Tell my father that I know he tried to save me. Tell everyone about what happens here."

Jacob felt Paul's hand on his shoulder, and then, walking tall, Oteka and Paul took long strides back across the village.

A brusque, guttural voice roared behind them. One of the

commanders was calling Hannah. There was much clamoring from the commander's tent. A fist hit the table. Jacob scuttled behind a hut. Hannah picked up the jerry can and ran.

Again Jacob made his way to the back of the tent that imprisoned Norman. He planted his feet firmly on the ground and in a swoop lifted his *panga* above his head. *Wait. Wait. Wait.* The radio blared. The noise was sudden and ear-splitting. *Now!* Jacob brought the *panga* down on the canvas. *Please don't let Norman be sitting too near.* The canvas ripped, more yelling, and the music was turned off. The commander was shouting once again. Oddly it was the commander's shrieking, not the music, that had covered the sound of Jacob slicing through the canvas. The yelling stopped. Then came a sudden slap, and Jacob knew that Hannah had been hit. *Don't think of that now.*

Gripping the sides of the tear in the tent, Jacob peered inside. Norman, wide-eyed and terrified, stared back.

Come, come, Jacob motioned with his hand. The boy did not move. *Norman, please*. Jacob mouthed the words. Could Norman see him? Frozen, the boy sat in the shadows. Jacob squeezed through the canvas wall, crawled across the dirt floor, and wrapped his arms around the boy. Norman's body vibrated and his teeth chattered as if he was very, very cold.

Outside the tent they could hear the commander continue to berate Hannah, his mouth full of foul language. The radio was turned back on.

"Listen to me," Jacob murmured into Norman's ear. "You must go back to where we were sleeping. Oteka and Paul are there. Norman!" Jacob shook him. The boy wasn't listening. "I will tell you something. If I had a brother I would like him to be like you. Smart. Good at multiplication. You are my war brother. We are in a war and we will win the war because we are the good, and good people win. Then you will be my peace brother. You must go now."

Still the boy did not move. Jacob grabbed him by the shoulders and gave him a shake. "Go!"

Tentatively, slowly, Norman nodded.

Jacob rubbed Norman's head and this time whispered into his ear, "Go."

Norman crawled across the dirt floor and soundlessly wiggled through the gash in the canvas wall.

Jacob waited. It was safer if they did not leave together, and he had to get Hannah. He counted off the seconds it would take Norman to cross the village. One hundred, two hundred, three hundred—finally Jacob inched his way through the slit in the tent and lay in the dust. The commanders were back to snorting and laughing, their fists pounding the table. The radio was playing louder than before. Again Jacob crawled to the side of the tent. The guard was still gnawing on a stick, like a small dog chewing a bone. Jacob peeked around the edge of the tent. Hannah had been knocked to the ground. She lay there, gulping back sobs, her face contorted with pain.

"Stupid girl," snarled the commander. Then he turned and pointed at Jacob. "You, bring us more soda."

Caught. Caught. Caught. It was over. Just like that. Every part of Jacob went dead cold. *Run, Norman, run.* Slowly Jacob stood. *Thank you, God, for this time on earth. Take care of my father.* With one foot poised to step out of the shadows, he stopped. The guard laid down his gun and stepped forward.

"Yes, sir," said the soldier. He saluted. "More soda."

There was no breath in Jacob's body and surely his heart had stopped. Not him, not him, the commander had not seen him. He eased backwards into the shadows and stood still—heart hammering, legs quaking.

"You. Get out of my sight." The commander snarled.

Whom was he talking to? Jacob saw the shadow of a black boot pull back. He winced. The boot hit Hannah in the stomach with a muffled *thud*. The boot drew back again, but this time Hannah rolled out of his reach. He missed. Jacob could see him clearly now, almost clearly. With one foot in the air and the other on uneven ground, the commander lost his balance. His comrades burst into hysterical laughter.

Jacob crawled to the back of the far hut to wait. Along the way he picked up his *panga*, stood, and held it in both hands. This time he would kill. If the commanders came after her he would, at the very least, kill one.

Come. Come. Come. Hannah, come. Jacob, wide-eyed, focused and ready, prayed.

And there she was. Half standing, half stumbling, wavering, soundlessly and wordlessly, she fell at Jacob's feet. Neither spoke as they listened for movement. They waited.

Nothing. The commander had gone back to his food. Now on hands and knees, pushing the *panga* ahead of him, centimeter by centimeter, Jacob crawled away from the tent. Hannah followed. They crept behind one hut, then another and another until they were at the edge of the village parade ground, the place where Kony had given his speech. His words seem to vibrate in this place. *"God is telling us that killing is right. God wants us to kill and we will do as God tells us."*

"Go, go without me. I cannot …" Hannah murmured.

She was clutching her ribs. She was breathless.

"Stand, you must stand." Jacob stood, then lifted her up as best he could. He wanted to put his arm around her to help her walk, but this was too dangerous. A boy was not allowed to touch a girl. Even in the dark they could be caught.

"It's no use. I think my ribs are broken. I will hold you back," she said, choking back tears.

"Try. Just try. I will walk first. Follow me." They had so little time. Soon the commander would notice that Norman was gone, and then there was no telling what would happen. The loud noise, the tear in the tent, the missing boy—the commander would put it together. These men were cruel beyond measure, hardly men at all, but they were not stupid.

Jacob turned and walked ahead. With her legs trembling beneath her Hannah walked. *God, God, help us now,* Jacob prayed. *Panga* in hand, Jacob walked tall. Unmindful of the sleeping bodies on the ground, of arms and legs, of little children curled up beside their mothers, he walked like a soldier. Soldiers did not care about girls and children, so Jacob tried not to care either.

Squinting, blinking, and peering into the darkness, Jacob at last saw Norman huddled under the tree. He touched Norman's shoulder and kept on going. Soundlessly, wordlessly, Norman stood and fell into step behind Hannah. Oteka and Paul were crouching by the path that led out of the village.

If they were right, they were five, six hours' walk from the safari lodge at Murchison Falls. *If* they were right. *If* they were on the right side of the river.

Without having exchanged a word, they were all now on the only unguarded path leading out of the village. Oteka went first. Behind him came Norman, Paul, and Hannah, with Jacob bringing up the rear. Between them they had one gun and two *pangas*.

Jacob looked back. Behind him were his classmates … Tony too. Was he a coward for leaving them behind? A deserter? He looked ahead, resolute, determined. Escape. That was what he had to think about. They had a good head start. No one knew.

But someone knew. Jacob turned back. He felt eyes upon him. Whose?

19
THE LION'S CLAW

In one hand Oteka held a gun and in the other he brandished a *panga*. They had left the path hours ago. Only when the underbrush became hopelessly tangled did Oteka use the long knife to cut a swath through the bush, and even then he did so carefully. No doubt their trail could be easily followed in the daylight, but the fewer signs they left the better. He was heading toward the river. His experience told him in which direction to go but it was his father's words that guided him. *"We do share a gift, my son. We always know the right path to take."*

The chirps of frogs and crickets reverberated in the night air. No one spoke. The code of silence was understood. They took long strides when they could and short steps when the ground became uneven or the bush closed in on them. Regardless, they walked in each other's footsteps. It was now a habit and, besides, it would be very easy to get lost.

The moon overhead illuminated the surrounding forest and each of them. Jacob looked up. It had been a full moon on the night the rebels stormed their school and took them from their beds. That was three full moons ago, three months. A lifetime.

Perhaps two hours passed, maybe more. Oteka motioned for them to sit. "I will climb that rock and see if I can get our bearings." He pointed to an overhang plainly lit by moonlight. Up he went, sure of his step.

Jacob and the rest sat down in the long grass to wait. Sitting among his friends, his family, Jacob felt calm. From the night of the abduction and during the whole of his captivity, he had been enveloped in a fog of fear, his whole being hurled into shock. Now his breath was even, measured, and he felt a purpose had come to his life—fear had grown into resolve and resolve into courage.

And then a surprise. Hannah undid the scarf that was tied tightly around her waist and revealed four fist-sized mangos. Paul could barely contain himself. He almost cheered. Hannah handed them out. They were hard as nuts and barely ripe enough to eat, but delicious all the same. The combination of tart and sweet seemed to fill Jacob's mouth. He had eaten mangos all his life but this was the first time he had really tasted one.

"This is the best mango I have ever eaten," said Paul.

And then he whispered to Hannah, "Thank you."

It was too dark to see her face, but Jacob saw her head and shoulders pull back as if she was astonished.

"Norman, are you all right?" asked Jacob. Norman had not said a word since Jacob had found him in the tent. The boy nodded but did not speak.

Oteka reappeared. "We are on track."

Jacob held out half a mango. He had taken one large bite, no more. Oteka looked at the fruit for a moment, seemingly unable to take in his good fortune. Then he ate. It was time to leave. This time Hannah tied the scarf around her head, covering her ears, or where her ears were supposed to be. *Perhaps,* thought Jacob, *she feels safe with us. With the LRA she used her disfigurement to protect her. Here, with us, she needs no such protection.*

Paul reached out to Norman, who was hobbling badly. The bigger boy and the smaller boy walked on. Jacob's feet were causing pain too but he had not said a word. What would be the point? Hannah let out the smallest cry, then hugged her middle with her arms. Jacob gently put his own arm around Hannah's waist. They walked. She leaned on him a little and he leaned on her a little.

Another hour passed. There was a distant sound, a far, far rumbling of thunder. But not thunder. It was too even, too consistent. Guns! Which way? Ahead or behind? They stopped to listen, heads cocked.

"Waterfall," Paul hissed. "Murchison Falls."

The sound of the waterfall grew louder with every step. Finally the five stood on a ridge and peered into a black abyss. They could hear the river below but they could not see it.

"There!" Oteka pointed to tracks that made up a sort of path down toward the water. Animal prints were everywhere.

Slip-sliding down the hill they followed the trail to the river's edge. They stood on trampled grass. Jacob sniffed. The river was foul and reeked. Thin rays from the moon winked off brown, sudsy water—animal pollution.

"What is this river?" Jacob asked.

It was Paul who answered, "The Victoria Nile."

Another terrifying sound and they all spun in their tracks. It wasn't a roar. It was a deep, menacing growl of something in anguish. Jacob's heart began to pound. Half-submerged eyes stared at them from the water—crocodiles, dozens of them, and all meters long. A crocodile, as gnarled and crusty as an old tree, blinked, then disappeared below the surface. One croc after another sank into the river. Hardly a ripple was left behind. But crocodiles did not growl. There was something else out there.

Oteka took the gun off his back, cocked it, and trained it on the surrounding bush. To fire would be madness—the sound would echo for kilometers. He would use it only if their lives were at stake.

"Look." Paul nudged Jacob. Upriver, great gray hippos lined the shore, hundreds of them. They moved like mammoth spirits from another time.

"Do not get between a hippo and the water," hissed Oteka.

"How do you know about hippos?" asked Paul.

"My grandfather," replied Oteka, and for the first time Jacob thought he heard longing in his voice. He trusted Oteka with his life, but really, he knew very little about him.

"Do you know where we are?" Hannah spoke in a low, muted voice.

"Oteka says that we are at Murchison Falls—the animal reserve," Jacob whispered.

Again Oteka volunteered to climb back up to the ridge and see if he could get their bearings. This time Paul volunteered to go too. The two set off.

Exhausted, and gingerly holding her middle, Hannah lowered herself to the ground, and Norman followed her lead. Jacob saw something move out of the corner of his eye. Then he heard it—a hiss. "Norman!" Jacob cried out. The boy leapt up. Jacob grabbed him, held tight, and looked over Norman's shoulder. It was hard to see but yes, it was a puff adder, a venomous snake. Disturbed, and annoyed no doubt, it slunk away. "It's gone now. It's all right," Jacob whispered into Norman's ear.

The boy's heart thumped so hard that Jacob could feel it through his shirt. "Rest. Rest." Gently Jacob released him and, still quaking, Norman crumpled onto the ground. Hannah laid her hand on the boy's arm. It was not hard to guess her thoughts, as they all had the same thought: danger was at every turn.

The three sat high up on the bank among the trees that lined the river's edge. Farther along, on sandy patches closer still to the water, crocodiles clustered. It took a few minutes but slowly the fright receded and Jacob became acutely aware of Hannah's presence.

What to say to a girl? And then, a thought. Hannah seemed to know all their names. How was that possible?

"Do you know about Oteka?" Jacob asked quietly.

"I was there when he was captured," she answered simply.

"Where did they capture him?" Jacob leaned in to hear her answer.

"He was walking on the road to Kampala when the rebels surrounded him. They called him a good catch because he is so tall and strong. But it was odd, he did not fight, and he did not look scared. It was as if he expected to be abducted."

A branch snapped. They caught their breath.

Paul tumbled down the hill, then stumbled toward them gasping for air. "Did you see?"

Oteka came running up from behind. "Move. MOVE!" he screamed.

Jacob, Hannah, and Norman leapt to their feet.

"Listen." Paul pointed in a different direction. "Footsteps."

Poised to run, they stopped, listening to the almost indistinguishable sounds. Not footsteps exactly, but the sound of something moving though the bush.

"Grab hold." Oteka flung his gun to the ground, seized a dangling vine, and hoisted Hannah up into a tree. She hardly knew what was happening but instinctively reached out and seized the branches above her head. Effortlessly Oteka lifted Norman next. The boy was as light as air. Norman climbed up into the tree and sat beside Hannah. Paul scrambled up another tree. All three clung desperately to thin branches. The trees were not strong, and the branches were brittle.

"Take this." Oteka passed his gun up to Paul. Only Jacob and Oteka remained on the ground.

"Pull!" Oteka yanked at more vines that dangled from the trees. "They must hold our weight."

Why? Jacob had no time to ask. Oteka had a plan, and Jacob trusted him; they all did. Frantically, furiously, with more strength than he had ever used in his whole life, Jacob pulled at the dangling vines. One vine after another gave way, but finally two strong vines held. Norman, halfway up the tree, reached down and further secured one with his hands. Paul, sitting in the tree, cocked his gun.

There it was again, that sound. "What is it?" Jacob was desperate.

"You go up." Oteka looked at Jacob. "It's coming."

In an instant, Jacob knew: they were being stalked, and Oteka was planning to lead the animal away from them. He said, "No, I am with you."

Hearts pounding, breath short, Jacob and Oteka faced each other in the dark. One was a rich boy and the other was poor. One was big, and muscular, with arms as thick as a good-sized tree branch. The other was smaller, and quick, with his strength in his determination. Now they were equals, both resolute, both stubborn, both firm. And then there was no time to argue.

"RUN!" Oteka turned on his heels.

"What is it? What is it?" Jacob ran behind.

"A lion. An old lion."

They ran. Oteka stopped to listen. Huffing, Jacob crouched beside him.

"Lions do not hunt people," hissed Jacob as he tried to draw air into his lungs. He knew little of wildlife but he knew that. He looked around. Which would be worse: to be eaten by a crocodile or by a lion?

"Old ones chased out of the pride hunt people, and this one is old and hungry. Listen." The two held their breath. Nothing.

"I hear …" muttered Jacob. And then, "I hear rebels."

"Double back. Run!"

"No … others … in danger." Jacob raced after him. But there was no other route to take. On one side, the river; on the other, a riverbank of dense bush; behind, rebels; and somewhere, the lion.

Oteka stopped. "The lion will come to the smell of blood." Oteka took his *panga* and held it over his arm.

Jacob stopped dead in his tracks. His bleeding feet!

The lion was tracking him!

"NO!" Jacob grabbed hold of Oteka's arm. "Listen." They turned toward a sound—someone running, coming up from behind. Jacob saw him first—red-rimmed eyes through the darkness. Lizard.

"Run!" Jacob cried. They dodged—left, right—then circled back toward the others, retracing their steps. Jacob's wounded, damaged feet left a trail of blood.

They heard Lizard shout an order to his men. "Do not shoot."

He was spent, exhausted, and yet still Jacob under stood Lizard's plan. He wanted Jacob and his followers alive. He would tether them with vines and march them back into the village. He would parade them in front of the whole camp. He would kill them slowly. He would be called a hero. He would become a full commander.

There was no screaming, no war cries, not from Jacob and Oteka, nor from Lizard and his soldiers. Every breath drawn into all their lungs was put to good use. Dodging, weaving, they thrashed their way back through the bush. Barbs and thorns, as sharp as knives, drove into Jacob's feet, drawing out yet more droplets of blood and pus. Their lungs might burst. And then—there! Ahead, copper eyes, jagged teeth, fur that shimmered gold in the moonlight. Jacob and Oteka spun on their heels, then looked up. Above in the trees, Hannah, Norman, and Paul waited with bated breath.

The lion roared, his body lengthening to cover meters of ground. He leapt.

The soldiers followed orders and did not shoot. Lizard shrieked. His soldiers scattered. Jacob dropped his *panga,* threw himself sideways, hands extended, and reached out for a vine. He twisted and turned, suspended and swinging. Norman and Hannah high up in the tree heaved and pulled, branches creaking and bending under the weight. Jacob arched his back and threw his legs over a lower tree limb.

Below, the lion roared and the screaming started. Upside down, head dangling, Jacob looked into Lizard's bloodshot eyes. In that split second he saw something—*the eyes of a boy, not a beast, just a boy.*

"Help me!" Lizard reached up desperately as the lion's jaws clamped down on his lower half.

"Paul, shoot!" Jacob screamed. Where was Paul? He had a gun; why did he not use it?

"Jacob!" Hannah screamed. "Jacob, climb higher!"

Using muscles almost forgotten, Jacob scrambled up into the tree. Hannah, Norman, and Jacob held onto each other as the lion ripped apart everything still alive on the ground. Where was Oteka?

Jacob cried out, "Oteka? Paul?"

The branches they sat on groaned under their weight. One wrong move and all three would plummet to the ground.

The screaming below was suddenly muted. Jungle chatter ceased. Nothing remained but the sounds of the lion tearing flesh from bone. Jacob, Hannah, and Norman sat still. Below, the earth turned red, and above, a white moon in a black sky watched.

Finally, nonchalantly, the lion dragged away his kill. Lizard had been reduced to a bloodied leg and shoulder bone.

"Oteka? Paul?" Jacob cried again but now his cries were more like sobs. *Please, please.*

And then came the answer, "We are here."

Jacob let go of his branch and landed on his hands and knees. The shock of it sent waves of pain throughout his battered body. One after the other, Paul and Oteka, too, dropped to the ground.

"Go," hissed Jacob.

Oteka took the lead. Paul went after him, then Norman and Hannah. They headed upstream toward the waterfall along the river's edge. Was it the right direction? Jacob was about to say something when he remembered his *panga*. The thought of going back made him want to retch. He kept going and then stopped dead in his tracks.

Lizard had a cellphone.

Jacob spun around and retraced his steps. They had not gone far. Soon the ground under his feet was blood- soaked. His mind and body told him to run, run away. Blood and bone mixed in with the damp muck. With his heart pounding he fell to his knees and ran his hands over the ground. If he could find the phone, their troubles would be over. *Father, to hear your voice again* ... There! He picked up a bit of metal. It was a belt buckle.

Anger seemed to swell up as he tossed it aside. His hands grew sticky with blood. The smell made him feel light-headed. He tried again and found what was left of Lizard's gun. And then he touched the cellphone. His hand shook as he lifted it to his ear. He pressed button after button. Dead. He yelled and pitched the phone against a tree. *God, why do You give and take back? Why have You forgotten us?*

He had to get away from this spot, had to run. There was a sound. What was it? Breathing? Someone was near. A rebel! Jacob dropped to the ground. Slowly, noiselessly, hand over hand, Jacob crawled around a tree. There it was again—sharp intakes of breath, almost as though someone was trying to stifle sobs. Jacob reached out and touched something metal. His *panga*! Gripping it in two hands he reared up and lunged toward the sound.

"Aaarrggh," he screamed.

"Jacob?"

As if suspended by mystical hands, Jacob came to a standstill, the *panga* still above his head.

"Jacob?"

He dropped the *panga*.

"Tony?" Jacob squatted down and peered into the shadows.

Knees by his ears, arms wrapped around his legs, eyes wide and silent, and his gun by his side, Tony was burrowed deep into the hollowed-out roots of a jack-fruit tree.

"Tony, come out." Jacob tried to quiet his own breathing. He gave his hand as a child would offer a bone to a puppy. Tony took it. In a flash, Jacob grabbed Tony's gun and slung it over his own shoulder. Tony did not object. He didn't even seem to notice.

"Tony, we cannot stay here." Jacob picked up the *panga* and both stood, walked, then ran silently through the bush along the river.

Oteka, Hannah, Paul, and Norman, standing near the water, looked back. Even in the moonlight Jacob could see fear on their faces. They expected one person and saw two.

"Rebels!" cried Norman. Oteka cocked his gun.

"It is me. It is all right. I am with Tony," Jacob called out. Fear turned into astonishment. It was hard to read Paul's face in the moonlight but nothing could disguise his behavior. He turned his back on Tony.

"Jacob," said Oteka. "We are on the wrong side of the river."

20
LIZARD

"I would rather be eaten by crocodiles or hippos than be captured alive," muttered Paul. No one disagreed.

"There must be a way across the river. We could build a raft?" suggested Jacob, but they all knew that that would take hours. They sat in silence. There were no tears, just overwhelming tiredness. They had come so far, only to fail.

"We can wait until dawn. Maybe we will be spotted by government soldiers," suggested Paul, but even as he spoke they all saw the flaw in the plan. From a distance, the government soldiers would think them rebels and open fire. And if the government soldiers could see them, likely the rebels would see them too.

"I know something," whispered Hannah. "At least, I think I know something."

All the boys leaned in to listen. Any idea would do, anything.

"When I was serving the commanders, they were talking about collecting the guns, the guns they wanted to trade Jacob and his friends for." Hannah paused. "I was not paying much attention, but they said that now that the deal was off they had no use for the boat."

A collective intake of breath was audible as each boy tensed up. Hope, they had hope.

"What else? Think, Hannah," said Oteka. It was the first time he had said her name.

"Just something about a boat that was to be left for them, to be used to pick up the guns. I'm sorry. That is all I know. I did not think it important at the time." Hannah's voice caught.

"No, it is good, it is enough." Jacob touched her hand. "It makes sense," said Oteka. "If Kony had plans to trade you for guns, then he must have had a way across the river to get them." He spoke while training his gun on the crocodiles and hippopotami that lounged by the water's edge. "Somewhere, there must be a boat, and it has to be on this side of the river. This is the most direct route from the camp. It must be near."

"The boat would be guarded," hissed Paul.

"Perhaps. We will have to split up and stay hidden. I will go west along the river. Norman and Paul, you go east. Count out one thousand steps and then turn back."

"I will go with you," said Jacob, as he smacked his legs and arms. The reeds by the river were thick with mosquitoes.

"No, stay here. The fewer people walking around, the less noise will be made," said Oteka.

This was true, but Oteka had also noticed Jacob's bloody feet. The lion had been tracking the smell of Jacob's blood. Soon Jacob would not be able to walk at all. Maybe they could carry him, maybe not. Hannah seemed to be struggling too.

And there was something more. Someone had obviously betrayed them. Someone had seen them leave camp and had alerted Lizard. In Oteka's mind, that person had to be Tony. Jacob might be blinded by friendship, and maybe even Paul too. Oteka could not trust Tony. Best that Hannah and Jacob rest, and watch over Tony.

"Come closer," Oteka motioned to Paul and Norman. They came together in a huddle. "We will climb back up the bank and walk along the ridge. Look for a freshly made path back down to the river. That is where the boat will be. And look for markings. Whoever left the boat would have left a sign, a signal of sorts."

All agreed to Oteka's plan. Jacob handed Tony's gun to Paul. They had two guns now, plus the *pangas*. Wordlessly, Paul grabbed the gun and, together with Oteka and Norman, climbed farther up the riverbank. At the top of the bank they split up, east and west. African elephants roamed the ridges of the river. Peaceful, lumbering, smart, they paid no mind to the searching boys.

Below, curled up in the roots of trees, Hannah and Jacob waited.

"Tony?" Jacob's voice was quiet. Tony sat on the ground, mute and glassy eyed, with his knees again pulled up to his ears.

"He is dead inside," said Hannah, "but his body continues to walk. It happens."

"No, not dead, sleeping maybe." Jacob inched closer to Tony. "Tony, listen to me. If we can cross the river, we can go home. It will be over." Jacob reached out to touch his arm but Tony edged away. Fear had vacated him and what was left was an empty shell.

"You are right to worry about him," said Hannah. "The commanders—they can tell which boys can be broken like glass. Shattered glass cannot be put back together. When the good boys become LRA they become especially mean, especially dangerous. I have seen it happen over and over."

"How do they know which boy to pick?" Jacob asked.

"Bullies always know."

Jacob sat down beside Hannah and ran his hand over his hair. The pebble in a leather pouch tied to his wrist bopped him in the nose. Magic stones that Kony had said would protect them from bullets—yet more proof that Kony was mad. Jacob ripped the pouch off with his teeth and threw it in the river.

"I have worn this so long, I had forgotten," said Hannah. She too tossed her stones in the river. Together they watched them sink.

"Did you ever ...?" Jacob stopped himself mid-sentence.

He had no right to ask.

"Did I ever kill?" Hannah spoke softly. "No. I was considered too useless to be a soldier. I was a slave and a servant, but because I served food I was able to steal and eat. I was never caught, not once." She spoke with pride. Jacob might have grinned in another circumstance; instead, he looked up into the night sky.

The dying moon kept ducking behind clouds, making darkness clamp down on them as tightly as a lid on a pot—then, in the next moment, it would be light enough to make out a face. In this country, in his Africa, it was possible to see Heaven while standing in Hell.

Jacob looked at Hannah from the corner of his eye. Under the thin band of material wrapped around her head were gaping dark holes. She would carry the scars forever, and if they survived, forever people would stare at her, nudge each other, and say that she was once a girl soldier. It would not matter if she'd killed or not. She would never find peace.

"If we live ..."

"We *will* live," said Hannah.

"What will you do?"

"I will join the nuns and become a teacher. It is what I planned. It is what I want."

They stopped talking for a moment and let peace settle. "Your feet ... thorns?" Hannah motioned toward Jacob's swollen, bloody feet.

Jacob shrugged. Try as he might, he could not dislodge the painful thorns.

"I will try." It was still too dark to see the thorns so Hannah carefully, gently, felt her way along. One by one she pulled out the slivers.

Jacob ran his hand along his soles. The thorns had been removed. "You would make a good nurse."

"I will make a better teacher."

"Yes, you will make a good teacher," agreed Jacob, and this time he felt his face crinkle into something like a smile. It was a strange sensation.

"I know the names of many children who were captured and killed. I repeat their names to myself before I sleep. One day, I will tell parents what happened to their children. One day, I will tell the whole world. If people know what happens to children like us, they will help."

Hannah seemed so sure.

Jacob had a thought. It was unlikely but, perhaps. "There is a man who comes often to my father's house. His name is Musa Henry Torac. His grandson was abducted, I do not know when. His name is Michael. Have you heard of him?"

Hannah, too shocked to reply, turned and stared at Jacob.

"Do you know of him?" Jacob repeated.

Hannah nodded slowly. "And so do you. Lizard. You know him by the name Lizard."

21
ONE SHOT

"We have found the boat." Paul was panting. "It's not far, and it's not much, but it should float. No guards, but the path is newly made."

Furiously smacking mosquitoes, Paul slumped down onto his haunches and took in a long breath. Norman, right behind him, did the same.

"And there are elephants up there, huge ones." Paul pointed up toward the ridge.

"A boat? How big?" asked Jacob. Six of them had to get across the river. The words *should float* were not especially reassuring.

"Big enough. We must go—now!" Paul stood again.

Jacob grasped a tree branch, pulled himself up, and looked down the shoreline. The crocodiles looked back. Dawn was not far away.

"Oteka has not returned," said Jacob.

"Go then," said Paul, still catching his breath. "I will wait here for him. Oteka and I can run. You will be slower. Norman, you guide them."

Norman nodded.

Paul had not yet looked at Tony, or even acknowledged his presence. Tony sat in a stupor, not sure of where he was or what was expected of him.

Jacob gently pulled Hannah to her feet. She cringed and took baby steps forward.

"Tony, come with us," said Jacob. Tony stood and followed.

"Norman, on the ridge, wait at the dying mango tree." Paul pointed up to a ledge above them, then turned to Jacob. "They used the tree to mark the path down to the river. It has been split with an axe. And Jacob, watch out for elephants."

Elephants? Jacob wasn't the least bit concerned about elephants. Crocodiles? Yes. Hippos? Definitely. Snakes? Absolutely. Spiders too. Mostly he was afraid of rebel soldiers. Did the commanders know that Lizard had left camp to track them? Or had Lizard set out on his own? They had no way of knowing, but either way, soon the rebels would come after them.

Norman, Jacob, and Hannah scaled the riverbank hand over hand then walked along the ridge in single file. The sound of the river and the feel of the path guided them. Jacob stretched his hands out to feel the dark. Hannah held onto the back of his shirt. The moon had almost died and the sun had yet to be born. *It is always darkest before the dawn*, Jacob remembered hearing. *It is the same with life*, thought Jacob. He felt the slightest jab—an *okuru-ogwal* bush! Hannah made it safely past, but Tony trailed behind.

"Tony, be careful," Jacob called. Too late, Tony stumbled headlong into it. Poisonous barbs pricked his skin. Tony seemed hardly to notice.

Predawn bird chirps and monkey chatter were beginning. Faster, they had to go faster.

"Look," whispered Hannah. The landscape ahead was open and barren. The silhouettes of lumbering, mountainous creatures appeared black against the faintly gray sky. They seemed majestic and calm. "Elephants are a sign of good luck," she said.

"Big rats, if you ask me," said Paul. He and Oteka had come running up behind.

One day, thought Jacob, *if we come out of this alive, I will ask Paul why he hates elephants.*

They came to the dead mango tree. Slip-sliding back down the bank, they stopped abruptly at the river's edge. There it was. It did not look very promising. Each of them squinted and considered. Once it might have had a small outboard motor, perhaps, but there was no sign of one now. It lay half submerged on its side.

"It might not be as bad as it looks," Hannah said softly, but there was doubt in her voice.

Oteka and Paul laid their guns on the ground and, batting tall reeds back with their arms, waded into the river. The front half of the boat bobbed in the current while the back half was mired in sand and rocks.

Jacob and Norman soundlessly placed their *pangas* on the ground and walked gingerly into the river, searching out flat rocks on the muddy bottom with their toes.

Hannah was about to follow them when Oteka called out in an almost inaudible hiss, "No, wait."

Jacob stood in the water at the bow. Oteka, Paul, and Norman took up positions and the four of them rocked the boat until they could heave it out of the sand and right it. They inspected it for damage.

"Look," said Paul. He was pointing to markings on the side of the boat. Most of the painted words had been scraped away but the letters *Sa* and *L* and *ge* were still legible.

"Sambiya Lodge," whispered Jacob. "This boat belongs to the lodge. It was left here deliberately for the rebels. They made it look damaged."

There were no holes in the bottom, or at least none that they could detect in the predawn light.

"Norman, get in," said Jacob.

Norman took hold of the gunwale and hauled himself out of the water. He fell, face first, into the boat.

"Oyi Maa! Maa konya! Maa munywala!" Paul hissed and pointed to dozens of leeches—long, slimy, black, and as thick as a finger—

that were welded to Norman's back and legs. Paul lifted a leg out of the water and let out a low moan.

Oteka stopped to listen. He had heard something. Animals? Rebels? "Hurry. Get back in the water. Shove off."

Norman leapt back out of the boat, his face twisted in revulsion. Hannah placed the *pangas* into the boat, then slipped on the slimy rocks underfoot and plunged into the water. Water flooded her mouth. Coughing, she found her footing. The harder they tried to be quiet, the more noise they seemed to make.

Tony slung both guns across his back, stood on the rocks, and made ready to push the boat off.

Again they rocked the boat. And then—*one, two, three, heave!*

As the boat slipped away from the shore, Oteka hoisted Norman back in. Tony, in a mad moment of awareness, made a giant leap from the rocky shore and sailed through the air to land with a thud in the bow of the boat. As the boat slipped into the stream, Jacob, Hannah, Paul, and Oteka fell face first into the filthy river water. Splashing—more noise! The current from the waterfall was weak along the shoreline but farther out, toward the middle of the river, the boat would be carried away.

Oars! Where were the oars?

Jacob was first to break the silence and called out to Tony and Norman, "Come back!"

Hannah, Jacob, Oteka, and Paul lunged toward the boat, gulping water. They beat the water with their arms. The splashing aroused hippos on the shore, which dove underwater to prance effortlessly along the bottom. Crocodiles, too, responded to the movement in the water. Early morning was feeding time.

Tony found something tucked under a thin strip of wood running the length of the boat. It was a sturdy pole, which he tossed to Norman, who stood at the bow. Norman—small, weak, starving

Norman—stuck the pole into the water until he felt it strike the rocky bottom. He put all his force into anchoring the boat with the pole, but he would not be able to hold it steady for long.

With broad strokes, Oteka reached the boat first and heaved himself over the side. Sputtering and nearly drowning, Paul lunged toward the boat too. Oteka found the oars and stretched one out across the water to him.

"Take it," he cried.

But it was Hannah, not Paul, who reached it first, with Jacob pushing her from behind. She grabbed hold, and Oteka pulled her in. Jacob kept his head above water until Hannah was safely in the boat, but then the last of his strength ebbed away. He lifted an arm, then slipped helplessly under the water. And he was gone.

The water was murky; it was impossible to open his eyes. He held his breath but began to sink. Through the stillness he could hear someone shouting his name. It was peaceful underwater. He had seen death so many times, looked at it, escaped it, challenged it, perhaps now was the time to die, perhaps it would not be so terrible. Everyone died.

Air bubbles dribbled out of his mouth and floated to the surface. He was not afraid. He had done his best. He thought of his mother and his father, of home, the farm. He even thought of Ethel and wished for her a husband. Someone, something, was moving toward him. He didn't care. He felt a powerful and mighty force come up from behind. He did not fight. Up he went, dragged to the surface. Arms encircled him. He was being pulled along. And then hands came down. Oteka, who could not swim, was in the water with him. It took Norman, Tony, and Hannah to drag him into the boat. Water spouted out of his mouth as he heaved, flapped, and floundered on the bottom of the boat before flopping over onto his back. He opened his eyes and saw fear on Hannah's face. Oteka pulled himself back into the boat.

Paul? Where was Paul?

A shot. Gunfire! Rebels? Government soldiers?

Instantly they all cowered down.

Standing at the stern of the boat, with a gun trained on the water, Tony put a bullet between a crocodile's eyes. Paul, flailing about in the water, was less than an arm's length from the crocodile's mouth. Tony dropped the gun, reached out, and pulled Paul into the boat.

Paul and Oteka tried to paddle. To row evenly together was impossible at first, then it became merely difficult, and after a few more minutes, possible. Norman held his position at the bow, and Tony stood at the stern, looking back, with his gun cocked. No one questioned his right to hold a gun. Jacob, still struggling to fill his lungs with air, did his best to collect himself.

The current was strong, and twice the boat veered to the wrong side of the river. The sun was not fully up but the sky had lightened. Just as day turns suddenly to night in Africa, so too does night turn suddenly into day. "Look!" Tony called out. Faces popped out of the bush on the riverbank. Rebels! They were standing on the spot where the boat had been launched. They had been minutes, mere minutes, behind them. A dozen guns were now pointed at their boat.

"Down!" They dove for the bottom of the boat. Its thin wooden shell would offer no protection from rebel guns.

The current was moving the boat along quickly. It was no longer possible to paddle without risking their lives.

"Why aren't they firing at us?" Paul's voice wobbled.

"Maybe we are too close to the government soldiers," said Oteka.

"Our Father, who art in Heaven …" Once it would have been Tony whispering a prayer, but now it was Paul. They all lay still and waited.

22
THE CROCODILE AND THE SCORPION

No shots were fired. Perhaps the rebels had received orders to leave the area. Perhaps Oteka was right and they thought government soldiers might be too close. Perhaps Kony was holding to the agreement not to attack on park land and frighten the wealthy tourists. Whatever the reason, when next Jacob peeked over the side of the boat, the rebels were gone.

The crocodiles and hippopotami were still there, though. The crocodiles on the shore basked in the early morning sun with their mouths wide open and the hippos wallowed in the mud. Above, tucked into the soaring cliffs rising from the river, birds swooped and nested, calling out to the day and each other.

Jacob slumped back down. The rebels would be on the march. And with them went the rest of the boys from the George Jones Seminary for Boys, likely lost forever.

Hours passed as the boat drifted along with the current. They tried to paddle but the effort was beyond them. The last food they had eaten was the small mangos many hours ago. The gentle rocking of the boat lulled them into a sleep of sorts. And then came a loud thud. Instantly they were awake and terrified. The boat had stopped moving.

Again Jacob was the first to look over the side of the boat. He expected a platoon of government soldiers, guns cocked, ready to kill. He expected to have his head shot off. At the very least, he expected to see a hundred crocodiles and hippopotami licking their lips, ready to eat them. He expected just about anything except what was in front of him.

"Look!"

Norman peeped over the gunwale of the boat. Oteka's, Paul's, Tony's, and finally Hannah's, heads popped up one after another. The boat was wedged between rocks along the shore. Another boat was anchored nearby. Only Oteka took in their surroundings. The rest gaped, open-mouthed, at the scene before them. Was it possible? Could they believe their eyes? They were at a dock of some kind.

Beyond the riverbank, in the middle of a grassy patch, sat a big, ancient gorilla, chewing on leaves. He gazed back at them with a perplexed stare.

"Is he harmless?" asked Hannah.

"He's very big and very old," whispered Paul.

"The lion was very big and very old too," hissed Norman.

"Apes don't eat people. They eat leaves." Oteka was relying on what he could remember of his grandfather's stories, told many, many years ago. In truth, he wasn't at all sure what apes ate.

"I did not think such beasts lived here," said Norman.

"You tell him to leave," suggested Paul.

Norman shook his head.

"One of us should get out and see if he attacks," whispered Jacob. Images of the lion tearing people apart crossed all their minds. None of the boys volunteered for the job.

"You can fight off rebels and lions, crocodiles and hippos, and you are all afraid of a big, fat monkey?" Disgusted, Hannah ignored her aching ribs and crawled out of the boat and over the rocks.

"Hannah. Come back!" cried Jacob. He should go after her. He should do something! But Hannah just scrambled down off the rocks and stood on the sandy shore. Head back, body erect, hands on hips, she looked dead-eyed at the ape. For all the attention the ape gave her, she might have been a stone. An interesting stone, a colorful stone, but a stone.

"Icoo maber?" Hannah spoke politely. She even bowed her head a little. *"Kop ango?"*

"Who is she talking to?" Paul sat back down in the boat. He couldn't look.

"The ape," replied Jacob.

"What is she saying?" Oteka put his head down too.

"I think she just said, 'Good morning, and how are you feeling?'" Jacob's voice rose in wonder.

"What's the ape saying?" asked Paul.

"Nothing so far," replied Jacob.

Step by step, Hannah tiptoed around the ape. Mildly perplexed, the ape watched her, but only because there was nothing else to watch. Finally she stood on the other side of the beast. With hands again anchored on her hips she hollered, "Are you coming?"

Tentatively, cautiously, sheepishly, all five boys scrambled over the side of the boat.

"Good morning." Clutching their weapons, each spoke with great reverence, hoping it might quell the animal's instinct to rip them apart, limb by limb.

Jacob looked the ape in the eye and felt the strangest sensation. It seemed human—more human than Kony and his band of soldiers ever could be.

"This is the road to the lodge," said Paul.

"Are you sure?" Jacob peered around. There were several sandy, rutted roads going in all directions. They could not afford to get lost.

Government soldiers would mistake them for rebels. Which road? Which way?

Paul pointed to the signpost overhead: "Sambiya Lodge, 2 km."

"Oh," said Jacob.

Oteka threw his gun down. "We must go unarmed."

Tony dropped his gun, too. Paul and Norman tossed aside their *pangas*. That was it; they no longer had any means of protecting themselves.

"I am the smallest," said Norman. "They might not kill me. I will go first."

Jacob looked at Norman and thought the boy looked old, almost wizened. A shrunken head on a shrunken body, not a ten-year-old boy any longer. But then they all had knobby knees and elbows, protruding bones, and gaunt faces. They were not *themselves*, not any of them. Jacob looked from Tony to Oteka to Hannah. If they survived the next hour, how would they go back to being the people they once were?

Shoulders back, head high, Norman the Brave walked down the middle of the rutted trail. One by one they followed, Jacob after Norman, and Oteka last.

"Stop!" yelled a disembodied voice. Guns nosed out of the tall elephant grass that grew along the trail.

They stopped. Hands in the air, they waited. *Please, God, please God.* Jacob could almost feel the bullets rip through his skin, almost see them dead and bleeding, sprawled out on the path like birds shot out of the sky.

"We are students of the George Jones Seminary for Boys. We have escaped the rebels." Norman spoke bravely and loudly, although his voice broke a little in the middle. "We want to come home."

23
RETURNEES

Returning home wasn't how Jacob had thought it would be. Twenty or more government soldiers leapt out of the grass as fast and as sure as great cats after a kill. They surrounded them, pushing, shoving, jeering, and snarling. One soldier babbled into a cellphone. Jacob heard the word *truck*. They didn't need a truck; they needed food!

"You took my sister!" hissed a government soldier. "She was walking to school. Where is she?" He rammed his rifle butt into Paul's back. Paul's mouth was clamped shut, his hands balled up into two rock-hard fists.

"Jacob?" Norman cried.

"They will not hurt us," Jacob whispered, but he was not so sure.

"Walk!" they were commanded. They all stumbled up the road toward the lodge.

Jacob looked over at Tony, who walked with his eyes fixed on the ground.

"You think that if you do not kill they will take you back? They will not believe you. They will treat you like a murderer." Tony's words rang in Jacob's ears. What if Tony was right? What if they would never be accepted again? What if they were forever blamed for all the things the LRA did? It wasn't fair, especially to Norman, a little kid.

Jacob wasn't mad, like Paul, or scared, like Norman. He was tired—*all* of him was tired, feet, bones, heart. His skin itched and hung off him like a shirt many sizes too big. His feet? No, he couldn't even think of his feet; he could barely feel them. They had made it, they had escaped, but here they were—still hungry, still afraid, still marching in front of guns.

"Hannah," Jacob whispered.

"Quiet." A soldier rammed the barrel of his gun against the back of Jacob's neck, just like before. Hannah did not look up. She, too, had her eyes glued to the ground while she secured the band of cloth covering her missing ears.

Paul, Tony, Norman, Hannah—they dragged their feet as if walking toward a firing squad. Only Oteka held his head high, like a prince, as if nothing could hurt him, ever again. Right. Jacob straightened up and threw his own shoulders back. This time he caught Norman's eye and made his mouth smile, as if to say, *It will be all right.* Slowly, as if each part of his body was working independently, Norman lifted his head and squared his shoulders too.

Good, thought Jacob. He looked at Paul and willed him to look back. It worked. Again, Jacob smiled. Again, he threw back his shoulders. Paul grimaced and did the same. *Good.* He turned to Tony. But nothing on earth could get Tony's attention.

A truck came barrelling down the road at breakneck speed. It skidded to a stop, kicking up pebbles and dust. A soldier opened up the back.

"Get in."

With all the dignity they could muster they climbed up into the truck and sat on a wooden plank, shoulders back, heads high. Only Tony folded up into himself, head down, slumped.

"Names?" Holding a clipboard and pencil, a soldier scribbled down first Paul's and then Tony's name. He came to Jacob.

"Please," said Jacob. "We need food."

"Name?"

"Kitino Jacob."

The soldier looked hard at Jacob, then reached for his cellphone. Soon after, each was handed a banana.

"Look." Paul touched Jacob's arm. Through the bush they caught sight of two women, one very thin and the other not so thin. One had hair the shade of sand; the other had lemon-colored hair. They were climbing onto a sightseeing bus.

Jacob nudged Oteka. "The government soldiers must be under orders to keep us out of sight of tourists."

Oteka nodded. He had been thinking the same thing. The truck lurched into gear. Jacob, Hannah, Tony, Paul, Norman, and Oteka sat facing the government soldiers and their guns.

The ride was three hours long, yet no one spoke. Mud huts, long grass, farms tended to and farms not tended to—all passed by in a blur of colors. And then, there it was! Gulu, his city.

The truck bounced in and out of potholes, tossing them from side to side, but Jacob couldn't help himself; he leapt up. The city, bathed in a waxy yellow light, seemed to beckon. Once, he had seen only blue, yellow, and red buildings. Now they were sapphire blue, saffron yellow, and rosy pink. And there were other colors, too—leafy green, burnt orange, and cinnamon brown. The buildings seemed to grow from out of the ground and sprout fully formed, beautiful to his eyes. *Boda-boda* boys zoomed about on their motorcycles, women went to market with chubby, well-loved babies on their backs, bicycles and smiles were everywhere—home!

The truck charged into town and rumbled down the main street. In front of the two department stores, and standing on wooden walkways, wire models displayed all sorts of *busutis.* Red and yellow posters advertising Bell Beer were plastered on the sides of buildings. Father always said that Ugandan beer was the best. Jacob's heart began to beat faster, faster, faster. *Never mind the government soldiers, never mind what people think. Father, I am home.* A shout from one of the soldiers made him sit down again.

The truck pulled into a large compound with gray cement buildings and stopped, jolting them all forward then back. There was no color here. Several boys playing football in an open, sandy space stopped to look at them. There were offices, a chapel, and a two-meter high wooden fence surrounding the entire area.

"Get out," hollered a soldier. Policemen were waiting for them.

Jacob heard the car before he saw it. The Honda Accord had barely come to a stop before Father flung open the door and ran toward Jacob. "Jacob, my son, my son," he cried over and over. He hugged Jacob, kissed the top of his head, then stood back and took in the sight. His eyes became wet; his voice grew quiet. "My son, I failed you."

"I will be well again. And you did not fail me, Father." He looked smaller than Jacob remembered, and older.

Father covered his eyes with his hands. Tears fell through his fingers.

A van pulled through the gates. Two nuns dressed in blue habits climbed out and hurried toward Hannah. Where had they come from? What did they want? Their arms enveloped Hannah and then the three walked back to the van together. What were they doing? *Stop! Stop!* The van doors slammed shut, and the sound echoed across the compound.

"I will be back, Father," shouted Jacob as he started to run across the compound. "Wait!" He could see Hannah's face in the window. He saw her mouth form his name. A policeman put up his hand. Jacob slammed into him as the van drove back through the gates. Hannah was gone.

The counsellors said it was best that they all stay in the rehabilitation center for a few weeks. Father argued. He wanted his boy home. In the end, Father relented.

The police interrogated them. They did not seem to care about how they were treated by the LRA. They only wanted to know about the guns and future plans of Kony and his crew. The boys exchanged looks. How would *they* know such things?

There were doctors, nurses, and social workers to tend to them, people who said that they must be reintegrated into society. They said that they must forgive themselves. Tony hung his head but Jacob could only wonder. Forgive *themselves?* They had been stolen, imprisoned, tortured, abused. Whom should they forgive? Jacob said nothing, so the rest followed suit.

They ate. They slept in single, squeaky iron beds. Norman especially slept a great deal. But Jacob would wake with a start at the slightest sound, his heart racing.

A week passed. There was a rooster in the courtyard that would crow at odd hours during the day, and sometimes in the middle of the night too, waking them when they had finally been able to get to sleep. At one point Oteka muttered something about throwing a rock at it, but they were all too tired to get out of bed.

■ ■ ■

"Tony, are you awake?" It was just before dawn. "Tony?"

Jacob got up, crept over to Tony's bed, and sat on the end. Tony rolled over and looked at the wall. He hardly talked at all. The counsellors said that it was normal; they said, "Give him time." But two weeks had passed.

"My mother is coming again today," he said in a low voice.

"That is good," said Jacob.

Tony's mother had come with his little brother the day after they'd arrived, but something had gone wrong. Tony's mother had yelled at the counsellors. "Demons!" she'd cried. "My son must visit the medicine man." She had shoved a packet of cream into a counsellor's hand. "Take this. It is *moo-yaa*, nut butter from a *yaa* tree. It must be smeared on my son's chest to cleanse him of his crimes."

"Your son is a Catholic," said the counsellor. "He does not believe in witchcraft."

More yelling. It went on for some time, and then Tony's mother and brother had left. She had not returned.

"They call her things, bad words, evil words." Tony's voice kept catching, like cloth on a jagged nail.

"Who, Tony? Who calls your mother things?" Jacob inched up the bed.

"The neighbors. At the well where she draws water they called out, *'Konyi pe.'* 'Useless,' they say. 'You are useless.' They shake their hands in the air and jeer at her. They know that I am a returnee. And my little brother, he is afraid of me. I can see the fear in his eyes."

The rooster crowed again and again. As Jacob turned his head to look out the window, Tony scrambled up and walked out of the room toward the latrine.

Paul sat up, rubbed his face, then put his arms behind his head and looked up at the ceiling.

"Would he have killed us, do you think, if he'd been ordered to?"

Jacob didn't respond. He just walked back to his bed and threw himself face first onto the mattress.

Returning home wasn't how Jacob had thought it would be.

24
A LIE FOR THE TRUTH

Father Ricardo looked uncomfortable. The priest from the George Jones Seminary for Boys sat in the courtyard, presiding over Norman, Paul, Jacob, and Tony like a *kwaro*, a grandfather. He looked down from his chair at the boys sitting cross-legged on the grass.

"Tony, God must have wanted you to experience the LRA for a reason. You will grow to be a better person, a better priest." As he spoke, sweat gathered in beads across his forehead.

Tony picked at the brown grass between his feet. "Paul, your athletic prowess has been missed."

Paul sucked in a breath.

He's thinking about Adam, thought Jacob. Adam, who had won the school races, who would one day have played for the national football team in Kampala, who might have tried out for the Olympic team. *He* was the one that the school missed.

Paul dithered, then spoke a little too loudly. "The night … when we were … taken," Paul's body shuddered, "I saw our teacher, Mr. Ojok. He was near the door, on the ground. Is he …?" He could not say the word *dead.*

Father Ricardo cleared his throat. "Mr. Ojok is no longer with us." He looked at the boys' astonished faces. "That is to say, he is teaching at another school. He was hit badly on the head. He has not fully recovered."

Father Ricardo mumbled something incomprehensible to Jacob, something about mathematics, wiped his forehead with his sleeve, then announced that he would visit again soon. He left the boys sitting cross-legged on the grass.

"I wanted him to tell us *why*. Why did the school let this happen? Where were our teachers?" asked Paul. The boys picked at the grass.

"Perhaps they too ran away," whispered Jacob.

Oteka, who had listened from a distance, walked over and folded his big frame down onto the ground.

"It does not matter," said Oteka. "Soon the reasons *why* will be forgotten and only the actions will remain. The deeds—good and bad—will be all we remember."

Tony stood up and walked back to their sleeping quarters.

Headmaster Heycoop, too, came to inquire about their health, and about the other boys—the ones left behind. He didn't look as formidable as he had when standing in the chapel and telling the students that they were the future of Uganda. He looked sad and uncomfortable. He had brought with him their suitcases from the school. The silver cases were lined up in the courtyard. They seemed out of place, from a different time. Finally, Headmaster Heycoop said that they were all welcome back at the school—that is, if they chose to return. He left in a hurry.

Norman's father arrived. He spent hours with the social worker, counsellors, doctor, and nurses before talking to his son. Norman waited on his bed to be called into the office. He was not gone very long. He came back into the dorm and, just like Tony, fell into his bed.

Jacob came over and stood beside his bed. "What happened?"

"My father said that he loved me, but he would not look at me. He is afraid of me, I can feel it."

"Norman?"

What could he say?

Oteka had no one and so he was not claimed.

One day, the counsellor handed Paul a letter from his father. Paul read it to himself, then he read it out loud.

"'Is there anything you want? What are your future plans?'"

There were many questions in the letter about the present and future but none about the past three months, about the LRA, about his experience in the bush. This was the father who had taken him to New York. This was the father who had said that he had great hopes for him! Paul folded up the letter and put it away.

Twice they tramped over to the hospital to see the doctor. The hospital was the biggest and the best in northern Uganda. It was made of red brick. Jacob, Norman, Paul, Tony, and Oteka registered with a lady in a little brick booth at the hospital entrance.

The receptionist peered at them over her glasses. She had heard about these returnees. Her upper lip curled. "The nurse will call you when the doctor is ready to see you." She motioned with her head to go inside.

The hallways were long and clean and open to the elements. In the middle of the hospital was a large patch of green grass. Families sat on the grass, and children played ball or slept under the trees. Wards surrounded this grassy area.

The wait was long. They grew hot under the sun. People watched them. Some patients came out of the wards to stare. Jacob tried to talk to a little boy who smiled at him, but the mother pulled him away.

Back from the hospital, they sat with their feet in the dust of the courtyard, their backs against the cement wall of their dormitory. Paul said out loud what they were all thinking.

"Do they think that we are killers? Do they think that we have a thirst to kill again?"

No one answered.

▪▪▪

"Jacob?" Father stood in the doorway of the room Jacob shared with Oteka, Tony, Paul, and Norman. Beside Father was Musa Henry Torac—Lizard's grandfather. Not since Jacob had peered down the barrel of the soldiers' guns at the lodge had he felt his chest tighten like this. The old man looked at him through bright, clear eyes. Hope, the man has hope, thought Jacob.

"Welcome home, Jacob," said Musa Henry Torac. "I prayed for your safe return every day, and now my prayers are answered."

Jacob, standing in front of the old man, nodded and tried to form the words *thank you.* His mouth felt as if it was sticky with glue.

"Forgive an old man for taking liberties, young Jacob, but even a short walk can leave me breathless. Come sit by me." Musa Henry Torac turned and walked back out into the grassy area and sat on a plastic chair.

Jacob looked around for support, someone to help him say what he needed to say, but Oteka, Paul, and Norman picked up a ball and wandered away. Tony, as usual, had walked off on his own.

"Are they kind to you here, young Jacob?" asked Musa Henry Torac.

Jacob nodded.

"You must know that you are a loved son, and that nothing you can do will change your father's love for you, or my respect for you."

Jacob looked over at his father, who smiled back at him.

"I know what happened to your grandson." Jacob blurted out the words. He had to say it now, quickly. He could hear Musa Henry Torac take in a sharp breath. "He is with God," whispered Jacob.

"Are you sure? You have never met him, never …" Musa Henry Torac's voice trailed away.

"I am sure. He was ..." Jacob dithered. *What is a lie?* Kony and his commanders had told lies over and over until all those around him believed. Anyone could be persuaded that a lie was the truth if they were told it often enough, if they wanted to believe the liar.

"Your grandson was a good boy. He was killed because he was a good boy. He did not suffer." Jacob looked the old man directly in the eyes when he spoke. In his mind's eye, he saw Lizard as he reached up to him, he heard his words: "Help me!" They were the words of a boy.

Musa Henry Torac nodded, his head heavy. "Yes, he was a good boy. Always kind. I loved him very much. I love him still. Thank you, Jacob. It must have been hard to tell an old man that his grandson is dead. The truth is important." Slowly he rose and left.

Father followed his old friend across the compound and through the gate.

The next morning they awoke to find that Oteka had slipped away in the night.

25
THE NATURE OF THE BEAST

"Jacob, I have news, good news," Paul waved a letter in his hand. "Tony and Norman got one too." He was jumping up and down now. "Look, see, Headmaster Heycoop arranged it. We will go to school in Kampala, and Tony's scholarship will be transferred. All three of us. No one will know us there. We can start again. We leave today."

Paul took a deep breath, as if to calm himself, then suddenly, almost mid-sentence, his voice grew soft and quiet as a murmur.

"I will take care of them in Kampala." Paul motioned with his head toward Norman and Tony. "It does not matter what Tony did. I will care for them like you cared for us."

Everything happened quickly. The staff gathered clothes for Tony. Instead of packing his things in a bucket he was given a tin suitcase just like the other boys. They took up a collection and handed him more notes and coins than he had ever held in his life. "This is for books and the things you will need." Paul and Norman repacked what little had been delivered from school. Their mattresses were bundled up with cord and stood propped up at the door, ready to go.

"Jacob, your father is sending a car for you shortly," said one of the counsellors. Jacob nodded.

"Jacob, what will you do?" asked Paul.

"I will go back to school. And maybe one day I will be able to tell people about us. Maybe if they knew they would help. It is what

Hannah believes." Jacob smiled. "I shall visit you in Kampala. Father goes there on business often. You will see, we will meet again," he said.

"Where do you think Oteka has gone?" Paul asked for the tenth time. Jacob shook his head. They knew so little about him. But they all felt the same way: with Oteka gone, something was missing.

Tony sat silently on his bed, his case packed. Jacob walked over and sat on his bed.

"Tony, it was not your fault." How many times had Jacob said that?

Tony shook his head as he picked up his bag. Norman let Tony pass out the door. The bus waited inside the compound.

Norman looked back at Jacob. He wanted to say something, to *do* something, but there were no words.

"What is 124 times 68?" said Jacob.

"Too easy. 8,432," replied Norman.

"I think that if we were in a multiplication contest, you would win," said Jacob.

"No," said Norman simply. Norman was getting better, day by day. "Goodbye."

And then they were gone. Jacob sat by himself. The room, so full of sounds a moment ago, became still. A lizard raced up the wall, and from somewhere far off he heard children playing football. The sounds were unmistakable—a foot meets leather, a cheer.

"Jacob?" Norman stood at the door. "I thought you had left."

Norman dithered. By nature he was a boy of few words, and many of those left to him were still held captive. He dropped his suitcase and walked over to Jacob.

"I think Paul has lied to us," he said. Jacob's eyebrows shot up in surprise.

"I think he told us those stories about America to make us think about other things. I do not believe children in America would be allowed to talk back to their parents, and I am sure children in America are not allowed to work the electricity," said Norman. "And I am very sure that Americans do not dress their dogs in clothes. I think Paul told us those things to ..." Norman searched for the words, "... to amuse us." Then he did something so surprising that Jacob took in a deep breath and looked on, amazed: Norman smiled. It was a beautiful thing.

"I do not know. I have heard many strange things about Americans and Europeans too," replied Jacob. "But I would very much like to go to America and see for myself." Norman laughed. It was an infectious sound starting way down in his throat and bubbling up like soda pop. And in that moment, swift and gentle, Norman kissed Jacob's forehead.

"Brother," he whispered.

This time the two walked out together. Norman, Tony, and Paul boarded the bus.

"There will be other returnees like you," said a counsellor to Jacob, as they waved goodbye. "More child soldiers will find a way out of the bush. *You* can help them, *you* can come back here and talk to them." The counsellor did not push, did not require an answer. Jacob nodded. *Yes, perhaps. Yes.* And then Father's green Honda Accord pulled into the compound and Ethel stepped out. She'd been skinny to begin with, and clearly she had lost weight. Still, she looked pretty. Jacob hadn't noticed that before, either.

"Come Jacob, let us go home," Ethel called out.

Jacob put his tin suitcase and mattress in the trunk of the automobile. "I would like to walk home."

"But ..." Ethel was about to argue. Jacob stifled a laugh. Could it be that she thought he could not find his way across the city he had been born in?

Ethel dithered, and then smiled. "You have grown. I will have to get used to this new Jacob. I shall have a Krest waiting for you when you arrive home." She smiled weakly, and that's when Jacob realized that she was just being protective. In her own way, she loved him.

"Thank you." Jacob shook hands and said goodbye to the counsellors and social workers before setting out on roads of red sand and scorched tarmac. His feet were still sore and he hobbled more than walked.

No one recognized him on the streets of Gulu, but then he was very thin. He peeked into kiosks, shops, stalls, and wooden lean-tos propped against crumbling buildings. He smelled the sweet scent of bananas sizzling on open grills. He gazed at the dried fish and papayas for sale. What he wouldn't have given for even a bite of such wondrous food not three weeks ago.

A feeling nudged at him. It had been there for a while. He pushed it down, back, away, but it kept returning, like the pain behind his eyes. Everything was the same, but different. He saw the colors, saw the beauty, but this city was not safe anymore, not completely. At any moment the LRA, or any army, could flood into the city like a torrent of rain and take him away again. He looked at the elegant women who passed him on the street wearing bright *busutis*, many with babies on their backs or tall bundles on their heads. Did they think that one day those babies could be taken away and made to kill?

He turned, walked through the courtyard, and entered the church through the side door. Jacob slid into a pew and looked up. "I'm back," he whispered to the baby angels painted on the ceiling. The pink *padi* bustled about the altar under the watchful eye of Jesus on the cross, and a woman sat alone near the top of the church in a pew, head bent. The only thing that had changed was Jacob.

"Why do such things happen?" he whispered. Jacob shut his

eyes. *Attack! Attack! Attack!* It happened like this. He would be fine, smiling even, and then memories would crash down on him like giant waves.

"Hello."

The waves turned soft and warm as the memories receded back to where they'd come from. He smiled, then opened his eyes and looked into almond-shaped eyes, at a nose and cheekbones sculpted into ridges, and a wide mouth made to smile.

"Where did you come from?"

Oteka slid in beside Jacob. "I have been watching the center for a while. I saw the bus leave with the boys, and then I followed you here."

Jacob nodded. Oteka had been taking care of himself a long, long time. Being confined and accountable would have been hard for him. "Where did you go?"

"I went back to the displacement camp, to a grave. I called her Adaa; she was an old woman who cared for me once as I cared for her. In the bush I felt her presence and strength with me always. She saved me, and I had to thank her."

Jacob understood. The woman at prayer crossed herself and left. Another woman took her place. The *padi* went away. A deacon in a white robe tied at the middle with a gold cord returned with tall candles. The two boys sat silently side by side for a while.

"Why did this happen? Why is it still happening?" Jacob asked the questions as much to Oteka as to the angels above, the statue of Mary in an alcove, and Jesus on the cross.

"Do you remember the story of the crocodile and the scorpion? You were here, the night in the church," said Oteka, his voice low. "I was out there, sitting on the ground. I could see you listening to the storyteller."

"I remember the story," said Jacob. "A scorpion rode on the

back of a crocodile across the lake. In the middle of the lake the scorpion stung the crocodile. As the crocodile began to sink he cried out 'Why? Why? You will die too.' Why did the scorpion kill the crocodile when it meant that he too would die?"

"Because," said Oteka, "it was his *nature*. It is what the scorpion was born to do."

A truck backfired, children called out to each other—around them there was peace, and just kilometers away, in the bush, beasts ruled.

"Are we born to be beasts? Is that our nature?" Jacob's throat closed up.

"No, we can choose. That is God's gift," said Oteka.

It occurred to Jacob that he would give his life for this friend, and yet the two had never talked, not the way friends talk. Was it possible to know a person's soul and not know the person? He did not even know if Oteka was a true soldier of the movement, if he had killed.

"I came to say goodbye," said Oteka. He looked Jacob in the eye.

Wide-eyed and amazed, Jacob looked back at Oteka. "But you've just returned!"

"When I was living at the displacement camp and taking care of Adaa, I went to a medicine man and asked him to contact my mother. I asked my mother, 'What is it I am supposed to do? What is my destiny?' I did not understand her message then, but now I do."

A chill came over Jacob. "What did she say?"

"Kony, my mother said *Kony*."

"She wanted to warn you. She wanted you to run away." It was obvious to Jacob, but something was whirling away inside him, something uncomfortable, not an idea but a feeling. Something bad was about to happen.

"I thought that too. I thought that if I stayed the LRA would raid the camp and I would be captured. I thought that if I left the camp and ran away, I would be captured on the road. I kept thinking, what was the point of telling me what would happen when I could do nothing about it? Before Adaa died she reminded me that my name meant 'hero.'" Oteka paused. Again he felt embarrassed but plunged on. "That's when I realized that all Acholi names have meanings. 'Kony' means 'save.' My mother was telling me to *save*."

"No, you cannot do this. This is madness. You will die," Jacob hissed. It was a loud sound that reverberated around the church. The deacon turned and glared at Jacob.

"I have Adaa's protection, and I feel my mother's and my father's presence too. And my father left me with a gift. He said that I would always know the right path to take and now that path is clear. I will help the government soldiers track the rebels." Oteka's voice was quiet, even, and resolute. "I will go back after the lost boys. I will save as many as I am able."

"I will come with you."

"I have watched you, Jacob. You are different now; you have found your voice. I heard you say to your friend Paul that you wanted people to know about us, to know what happens to child soldiers. So tell them. You have great things to do in your life. You must follow your destiny, and I must follow mine. I know the voice of the true God. I will follow that voice. It is *my* nature."

▪▪▪

The road out of town was the same road that passed by Jacob's home, and so the two walked together through Gulu. They stopped at the entrance to Jacob's family's compound.

Jacob dithered and pondered but in the end he came out with

his thoughts. "Oteka, I must ask and I am sorry." And here Jacob paused. "Did *you* kill?" Was the question fair? Did he have the right to ask?

Oteka did something surprising. He laughed. "The commanders are greedy. They cared too much for well-cooked food. When I was sent into battle it was not to kill; it was to make sure the other soldiers did not steal the food they found in the villages. They wanted me alive so that I could return and cook their food. No Jacob, I did not kill."

"Would you have?" It was hard, but Jacob looked Oteka in the eye.

"You are not asking *me* the question, Jacob, you are asking yourself. I hope one day you find your answer.

"Brother." Oteka and Jacob clasped hands.

"Brother," said Jacob. "I will see you again."

As Oteka walked away he should have become smaller and smaller in Jacob's sight, but instead he became bigger and bigger, until he filled the whole skyline.

"Jacob!"

Ethel stood, hands on her hips, beside the guardhouse. The guard himself was tucked away in his little wooden hut. Jacob grimaced and walked toward her, but not before taking one last look down the road. Oteka was gone.

"Welcome home." There might have been a hint of a smile on Ethel's face because when she moved aside Hannah came into view. Jacob took a breath. She wore a simple dress. A band of colorful material covered her ears and her hair was done in strange, thin braids looped up and around, creating a sort of halo. Her eyes were wide, her nose thin, her mouth curved into a gentle smile. She was—Jacob could hardly speak—not pretty, but *beautiful.*

Ethel looked from Jacob to Hannah and sighed. "I shall leave you two, but after you have said hello, go and talk to your father. He is under the mango tree." Off Ethel went.

They waited until she went into the house before they spoke.

"She is very bossy." Hannah giggled.

Jacob laughed. "That is because she loves me. Where have you been?"

"Did you think I would go away forever?" she asked simply.

"Are you a nun?" He blurted out the question. Why did he keep doing that? He did not know how to talk to a girl. How, then, was he supposed to talk to a nun?

"No, I am living with the nuns and I am studying to be a teacher." She gazed at him with a steady eye.

"Will you … I mean, might you ever become a nun?" There, he'd said it, and now he would be happy to sink into the sand.

"I do not think it would be right for me. I stay with the nuns because I have no family." Suddenly shy, she looked down.

"You have family." Jacob's heart pounded so hard it made hearing difficult. Speaking was almost impossible. All he could manage were the words, "Come and meet my father."

Jacob and Hannah walked into the garden toward the great mango tree. It was a sweet–sweeter life.

GULU, UGANDA, 2009

Dear Reader,

As best I can tell it, this is our story. Many years have passed, and I would like to report that Kony and his Lord's Resistance Army no longer exist, but that would not be true. I have never quite gotten over the feeling that although Kony has lost much of his power, he still lurks in the bush, hides behind huts, and prowls in elephant grass, ready to pounce.

To think back to those times still causes me anguish, but it has brought some insight, too. I remember Michael, the boy called Lizard. Hindsight allows me to see that he was as much a victim as an enemy. But that is the question that we all wrestle with—where does the victim end and the criminal begin? Who is accountable? Child soldiers are instruments of evil men. How can we punish the child? What happens when the child grows up and continues on the path of murder and destruction? The world will see many more such children. It is a question that must be answered.

But perhaps you would like to know about the rest of us. Again, I would like to give you only good news, but that would not be honest or true. We all still suffer from that hateful time, some more than others, and all in different ways.

Tony did not find a way to absolve himself for Adam's

murder or his betrayal. I believe he saw us escape that night in the bush. Judas betrayed Jesus. In Tony's mind betrayal is the greatest of sins. As his great friend I forgive him and wish only that he could have found a way to forgive himself.

Not surprisingly, Tony did not become a priest. He left school almost a month after he and the others arrived in Kampala. Paul did his best to live up to his promise to care for him. Twice Paul set out to find Tony in the twisty, often dangerous slums of our great capital city. Twice Paul brought him back to school. Finally, Tony left for good, and no amount of cajoling or imploring could change his mind. Still Paul did not give up. He would sneak out of his dormitory to bring Tony what little food he could scavenge and shared his meager allowance with him. As time went on, Tony became more wild and reckless. He died of AIDS last year in Kampala. My country will miss the man he might have become. I will miss him forever.

Paul is studying engineering at Makerere University in Kampala. He will carry on his studies next year in England at Bristol University. When he is in England, he says, he will take pictures of dogs and cats wearing clothes. Norman still does not believe that such things are possible. Paul is successful, but his scars are within. He does not speak regularly with his father or the rest of his family. I remember the night at school when he first told us about his trip to America. He tried to hide the pride he felt for his father, but it was obvious. Paul says that his father now avoids him. I think that this has brought him great heartache. To live without family is to be alone. Paul is always busy. It is as if he is afraid to stop walking, walking, walking. I have never asked him why he did not use the gun to shoot the lion. Perhaps it was too dark to see. Perhaps his hatred for Lizard ran too deep. Perhaps I do not want to know the answer. And, I have yet to ask him why he does not like elephants. Maybe I will remember to ask at our next meeting.

Norman is now seventeen years old and completing high school. He hopes to go on and do a physics degree in university. He visited Gulu last year. Hannah says that he is a handsome boy. I trust her opinion as I might not be a good judge of such things. But he is still quiet and given to reflection. We have tried to talk about our experiences with the LRA but even the mention of it brings tears to Norman's eyes. When that happens, I too am transported back to the time when I tried to make shoes for him out of banana leaves and vines. I think that had we competed in a mathematics competition, he would have won.

I hope this news will bring a smile to your face. My father and Ethel married last year. They live in Pader District on the farm. Ethel is still bossy, but I know she cares deeply for my father.

Hannah is a teacher, and here is another surprise. We are to be married within the month. It took a long time to convince her that I was the right man for her. Father cares for Hannah very much. He searched for Hannah's extended family so that he could pay them the traditional bride price. Sadly, he found none. This is not usually the case in Africa, but then AIDS, disease, and war have taken a heavy toll.

Since Father cannot pay Hannah's relatives the bride price, he has decided to give Hannah herself many cows. This is very unusual, but my father is a very unusual man. My soon-to-be wife is now a rich woman. I can tell people that I am marrying Hannah for her wealth!

The wedding preparations are going on as we speak. Since Hannah does not have family, Ethel has put herself in charge. Hannah is trying very hard not to lose her temper. I have little to do with the planning but my greatest wish would be to see Oteka at my wedding.

We will live in Gulu in this house, my childhood home. Next year we will visit America. We will first go to England and see the Queen from a great distance. Even now I hear my mother's voice.

Pussycat, pussycat, where have you been?
I've been to London to visit the Queen.

We shall see the snow in Canada, although the thought of snow frightens Hannah terribly. We will also see the famous lights of New York City. What will it be like? I can only imagine. And then we will come home. Uganda is where my heart resides and I could no more live without my country than I could live without my heart.

Perhaps this sounds like too much of a happy ending, and perhaps it is. With the exception of Tony, we are alive and we go on while so many have died or remain captive. But there are still costs. I suffer from extreme headaches that leave me quaking in the dark. We all have moments when memory becomes real, when the world we *can* touch and the world we *cannot* touch collide. There are times when I am sitting here at my desk and looking out at the mango tree where my father once sat and suddenly I hear, "Attack! Attack! Attack!" I hear gunfire and see blood bloom like a red *ature* flower in the middle of a chest. I see sunlight glint off a *panga* blade and severed limbs on the ground. And when these visions occur, my hands shake while the rest of me goes rigid. Soon I am soaked with sweat.

Hannah, too, experiences such moments. I have seen her suddenly grip a chair or a table to prevent herself from falling. I see her eyes grow wide, her teeth and hands clench. She touches the band of cloth around her head, then waits for the moments of terror to pass. After all these years, Hannah still has not talked about her war sister, Sarah. Nor has she ever spoken about the incident that resulted in her torture. I do not believe that she ever will. We help each other as best we can. You should know, I will love and care for her until I die.

Once, and perhaps this is funny, I was walking through the kitchen. Grasshoppers waiting to be cooked were popping in a covered pot. *Pop, pop, pop*. I fell to my knees in terror. Poor Bella. She has banned grasshoppers from the kitchen but does not know why. I cannot explain. She is very old now and it would hurt her if she knew too much.

I have saved the hardest news for last. Hardest because it causes me pain to write it. Oteka spent years in the bush rescuing girls and boys, including some boys from my old school. After many long and dangerous treks he would arrive here at the house. We would talk late into the night about God and if He hears the voices of the lost boys and girls in the bush. Long gone are the days when Oteka would visit a medicine man. Oteka is now a committed Catholic trying to do God's work.

We tell the story of the crocodile and the scorpion over and over, then debate and wonder: Are we all beasts inside? What is our nature? Can a good boy be turned into a killer more easily than one who was not a good boy in the first place?

I think of how the words of God were so misused by Kony and his commanders. I now believe that if you tell a lie, feed it, nurture it, and help it grow, it will be believed. It will grow powerful despite being rotten at the core. Our talks were long and passionate.

Two years ago Oteka went off in search of more lost boys and girls. He has never been away this long. There have been reports of a gentle giant felled near the Congo border. Others have said that a very tall young man was seen walking toward the Sudan.

In my mind's eye I see his towering frame protecting us. I feel the warmth of his smile, and I live in hope that one day he will return. Always there is hope. Hope for Oteka. Hope for child soldiers. Hope for all of Africa, the cradle of civilization, home to eight hundred million people, birthplace of the written word. Hope for my country, Uganda.

Jacob

AFTERWORD
BY ADRIAN BRADBURY

War Brothers is fiction. The war in northern Uganda is not.

It is a fact that, for well over twenty years, the Lord's Resistance Army (LRA) has fought the Ugandan government, and at the same time terrorized two million innocent civilians.

It is a fact, as you have read, that the most horrific of the LRA's crimes has been the abduction of as many as sixty thousand children, who have been used in this war, against their will, as soldiers, laborers, and sex slaves.

And while these may be facts, they are not statistics—they are children.

They're kids, just like you.

They dream about being a doctor, a teacher, or a professional soccer star. They dream, however, between nightmares of their time in the bush. They dream of the terrible things they have been forced to do, or they too would have been killed.

While it's difficult for us to comprehend, they are the lucky ones. There is an entire generation of kids that has not lived even one minute of their lives in peace, and they are the lucky ones.

Take a minute and think of the last time you were really afraid, say, when you were caught in the dark and panicked. Now imagine what it might be like if that was how you felt every single day.

When we started GuluWalk, with the support of so many volunteers worldwide, we did everything we could to play a part in peace for Uganda. We focused every minute of every day on supporting the abandoned children of northern Uganda.

And even with relative peace, there is still so much more we all can do to raise our voices and be partners in the future of the Acholi children.

It can seem overwhelming—and I'm sure you'll ask yourself, "How much of a difference am I really going to make? I'm just one person. What will it matter?"

Just ask yourself this: "What would Jacob do?"

Adrian Bradbury is the founder of GuluWalk, a campaign that started with the footsteps of just two people and grew into an urgent and impassioned worldwide movement for peace. GuluWalk took place in over 100 cities in 16 countries, and raised over $2.5 million for the children of northern Uganda. Today, Adrian is providing opportunity for youth in the region through sport and the Gulu United Football Club. For more information or to find out how you can get involved, please visit www.guluunited.com.

GLOSSARY

Acholi: Ethnic tribal group prominent in northern Uganda.

***Adaa*:** Grandmother, a term also used to show respect to an elderly woman.

AIDS: Acquired immune deficiency syndrome; also called *twoo jonyo*, or *kisipi*, or *cilim,* the slimming disease.

***Ajaa*:** Bells.

Amin, Idi: A monster who gave his country an eight-year reign of terror (1971–1979). During Amin's time in office, three hundred thousand Ugandans were murdered, many of whom were doctors, the elite, and the educated.

***Angut!*:** A curse word whose meaning depends on the context of its use. Here, a simple translation is "Serves me right" or "What have I gotten myself into?"

Ankole cattle: Domestic, longhorned cattle with a long head, short neck, and narrow chest. The male often has a thoracic hump. The length of its horns and its coloring often determine the value of the cow.

***Arege*:** Local moonshine or homemade alcoholic drink.

***Atoo tin!*:** This phrase must be translated in context to the situation. Here it means roughly, "I'm dead today." In Western terms think, "Just shoot me."

***Boda-boda*:** Motorcycle-taxi or bicycle. People in need of a lift flag one down and hop on the back.

***Busutis*:** A traditional wraparound dress, although not necessarily of the Acholi tradition.

Cassava: A tuber root that may be eaten fresh or dried, or may be turned into flour. It is an African staple but has minimal nutritional value.

***Cen*:** Evil spirits.

***Cilim*:** AIDS.

***Do-do*:** Green vegetables.

Football: In North America, we would call the game they play in Uganda *soccer*. As an example, in the British tradition a *football* is what we would call a round *soccer* ball.

***Gagi*:** Shells.

***Geuka*:** Right (direction).

***Jogi*:** Witches, spirits.

***Kabutu*:** Sleeping place; it is sometimes a bit of wood raised on the ground, or other times an animal skin laid over hard ground.

***Kisipi*:** AIDS.

***Kisra*:** Sorghum bread.

***Kolo*:** A mat outside the hut.

Kony, Joseph: Leader of the Lord's Resistance Army (LRA).

***Konyi pe*:** A derogatory phrase often shouted at the mothers of child soldiers who have returned. It translates as "You are useless."

***Kwaro*:** A grandfather.

***Lacoi*:** A milky white drink, thick and potent.

***Lajok*:** A witch doctor with great and evil powers.

***Lamero*:** A drunk.

Langi: An ethnic tribal group prominent in northern Uganda.

Language: The official language in Uganda is English, although it is not uncommon for a child attending elementary school to speak English plus two or three local dialects, along with KiSwahili, Italian (due to the influence of the Catholic Church), and perhaps French.

LRA: Lord's Resistance Army.

***Lwit oput*:** A herb that is reputed to reduce pain.

Maize: Corn.

***Mak wot*:** Walk faster.

***Matooke*:** Steamed and mashed banana.

***Mazungu*:** White person.

Medicine man (Sometimes called *ajwaka.*)**:** In the very simplest of terms it is believed that a medicine man can communicate with spirits; use local medicines for healing purposes; identify or chase away evil spirits called *cen, ayweya, gemo,* or *jok;* and commune with the spirits of the dead.

Money: 1,700 Ugandan shillings are roughly equal to $1.00.

***Munu*:** White person.

***"Munu, mina cwit!"*:** Children's saying that means "White person, please, give me candies."

Murchison Falls: Flanks the Victoria Nile, 300 kilometres northwest of Uganda's capital city, Kampala.

Museveni, Yoweri: President of the National Resistance Party (NRM), 1986 to the present time. Under this regime, Uganda has seen a re-establishment of law, an appointed Human Rights Commission, increased freedom of the press, and the establishment of a publicly funded elementary school education (to Grade 6).

***Mutoka*:** Jeep, motor car, or automobile.

***Nyuma*:** Left (direction).

***Okuru-ogwal*:** Flowering poisonous plants often used around the outside walls of a house to deter thieves.

***Ongere*:** Young squirrel.

***Otidi*:** Small.

***Owii*:** A type of tree.

***Oyot oyot*:** Hurry.

***Padi*:** A priest.

***Panga*:** A long knife or machete.

***Pekke*:** Small box or bag containing food.

***Potio*:** White cornmeal.

***Sapatu*:** A flip-flop sandal.

***Tipu*:** Prophet, holy one.

***Tong*:** Spear.

***Twoo jonyo*:** AIDS.

White ants: In Acholi, called *ngwen.*

***Woda*:** "My son." The Acholi people, especially older women, might call any younger man *woda* out of respect.

ACKNOWLEDGMENTS

My sincere thanks to: Thomas Edward Otto, LL.B., a Ugandan Canadian currently enrolled to be licensed as a barrister and solicitor by the Law Society of Upper Canada; Opiyo Oloya, a school principal and Ph.D. student originally from Gulu, Uganda; Akullo Evelyn Otwili, a translator and university student in Gulu; Okello Moses Rubangangeyo, a former lieutenant and brigade administrator officer (rank while in captivity in the Lord's Resistance Army, LRA); and to those in the NGO offices in Gulu who helped in many ways. Thank you.

If this book has any merit, if it resonates at all, it is because of Catherine Marjoribanks' careful and dedicated editing. With all my heart, thank you Catherine.

Thanks to Ann Ball, Donna Patton, Shelley Grieve, and Linda Bronfman, great friends who said what they thought and damn the torpedoes.

And thanks to Hannah Grieve, Holly and Jack Caldwell, John McNally, Kimberleigh and William Sparrow, Jeremy Hlusko, and Melissa Bellm. Then there is Mary Askwith, who put up with her mom gabbing on the phone for hours. (Mary, she was talking to me.)

Thanks to Julia Bell, intrepid and fearless traveler to Uganda.

Thanks to Adrian Bradbury, founder and director of GuluWalk and darn fine travel agent.

Thanks to Ian Elliot, *Different Drummer*, Burlington, Ontario, who searched the world for reference books; Katie Hearn at Annick; and copy editor Laurel Sparrow, a late comer to the project but very welcome.

And finally thanks to Laurel, Kai, Sam, Joe, and David.